# An Orion Anthology

Compiled by:

Roy L. Wachter

Copyright © 2015 Roy L. Wachter

All rights reserved.

ISBN: 1514741830
ISBN-13:9781514741832

*Blah, blah, blah* © 2014 Name Name Used with permission
"Blah, blah, blah" © 2015 Name Name

Note: This book is a compilation of works of eighteen authors. Although this book is copyrighted, individual authors and illustrators maintain intellectual ownership of their work.

The small town of Orion lies nestled among rolling hills that are populated with century old maple, oak, and sycamore trees. This fictional town is similar to many of the small towns scattered over the south central Indiana. This town could be or perhaps should be your hometown. The town is named Orion after the zodiac constellation, *Orion the Hunter*. For that reason, local sport teams call themselves Hunters.

Eighteen authors from Daviess and Knox counties in Indiana have written a variety of poems and short stories about events or happenings in or near Orion. Some are humorous; some are dramatic, but all are interesting.

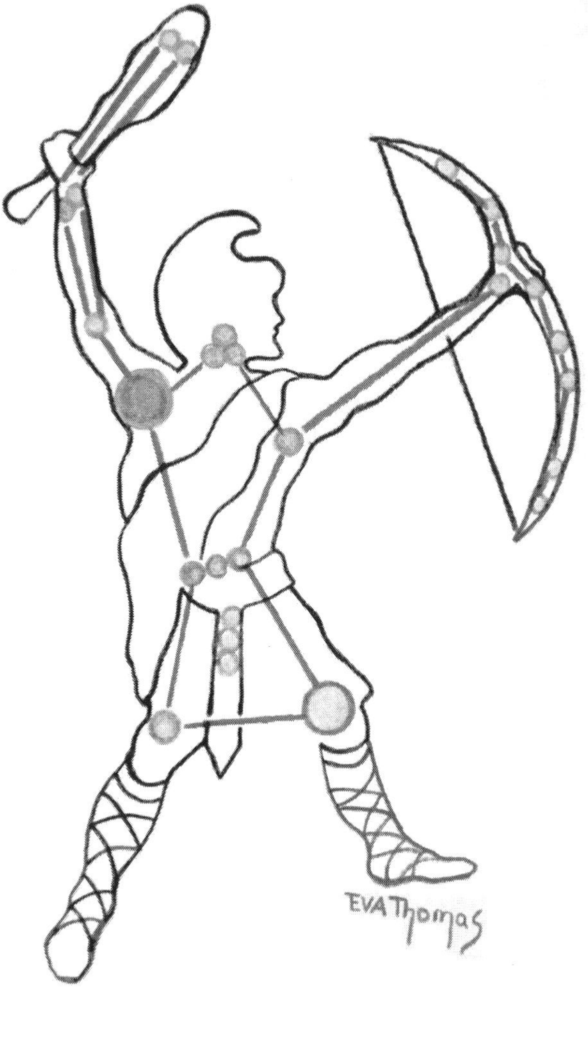
EVA Thomas

## CONTENTS

| Title | Author | Pg# |
|---|---|---|
| New Country | Julie Lancaster | 1 |
| Binoculars | Roy L. Wachter | 7 |
| Vincent Price, Rabbit Ears, and Snow Bunnies | Kathi Lengacher | 15 |
| I'm My Brother's Keeper | C. B. Buckley | 23 |
| Big Bird | Amy Gardner | 27 |
| Return to Orion | Roy L. Wachter | 29 |
| Fill My Cup | Wini Fagen Frances | 43 |
| Notes from the Other Side of the Circulation Desk | Erin Maley | 45 |
| The Catalpa Tree Squirrel | Amy Gardner | 53 |
| Do You Believe? | Pauline Mangin | 55 |
| The Christmas Medal | C. B. Buckley | 57 |
| The Undecorated Christmas Tree | C. B. Buckley | 59 |
| Bambies | Amy Gardner | 61 |
| Broken Promises | Brooke Kavanaugh | 63 |
| Silent Night | Mary B. Goss | 67 |
| Thank You | Vince Sellers | 71 |
| Potato Bugs | Roy L. Wachter | 75 |
| Rainy Days | Larry Mattes | 77 |
| The Rainmaker and The Preacher | Connie Carroll | 79 |
| Duff, My Home Town | Gordon Hochmeister | 83 |
| Fifth Sunday Surprise | Wini Fagen Frances | 89 |
| Straight from The Cow's Mouth | Blake Chambers | 93 |
| Conscience | C. B. Buckley | 103 |
| Murder in Meeting Room Three | Molly Daniels | 105 |
| Aston Oakes | Amy Gardner | 113 |
| The Mouse House | Georgia Prewett Buckley | 117 |
| Orion | Floyd Root | 125 |
| Ghosts of Home | Wini Fagan Frances | 127 |

# ACKNOWLEDGMENTS

The authors of Orion Anthology want to thank the following friends for their assistance:

| | |
|---|---|
| Julie Bassler | Digitizing Illustrations |
| Grace Bassler | Digitizing Illustrations |
| James M. Bowers | Basic Formatting |
| Joan M. Colbert | Editing |
| Eva Thomas | Illustrating |
| Floyd Root | Locating Formatting Service |

# NEW COUNTRY
## Julie Lancaster

Loud chatter filled the air in the Naples airport terminal in southern Italy. Eighteen-year old Elena Spango, nervous and excited, was preparing to board the massive jet for the USA. She was leaving her loving family and home in Italy for a new life in America. For such a young woman, recently graduated with honors from high school, this was a huge event. It was also a series of firsts: first of her family to leave her country, first to go to college, first to become an engineering student anywhere, especially in America! Elena was going to Indiana, far from all that was familiar to her.

The question must be raised: How did this all come about? Not surprising are the answers! Elena was loved and supported all her young life. Her parents Giacomo and Sarafina Spango were traditional and hardworking farmers, who recognized their daughter's abilities and encouraged her. Elena had a talent for languages, could speak fluent English, excelled in math, was involved with her community, and had boundless curiosity, and a love of adventure. She was also very hard working and had dreams. Her parents encouraged to follow those dreams, rather than remain in the typical role of Italian girls of keeping the "Famiglia" intact.

But staying was not going to be the norm for this young woman. Although she was terrified to take such a risk, she was more excited and determined to face the challenges before her. As it turned out, success was inevitable for her. She adjusted well to the USA and to college life. Because she was so friendly and outgoing, she quickly became a favorite among her fellow students. She was the only Italian in the program and gained much respect. She was lovingly referred to as the "Eyetalian." Among her many friends was the engineering student, Jim Bradford. He was kind and supportive of her. Their friendship grew into love, and they thrived throughout their college years. But, eventually Elena had to make an agonizing decision: would she stay in Indiana and marry Jim or return to Italy where all her love and support resided. Could she survive in this new country, build a life here, abandoning everything she knew and loved in the old country? Could she assimilate and become part of this new culture and not look back?

This was a great dilemma. Although she knew her priorities, she also knew she could balance them. She had been returning to Italy twice a year. She brought Jim with her, which helped to transcend the cultures. But most of all, she got her parents blessings to pursue her life. It looked like southern Indiana would become her choice for life. And so, Elena and Jim made the commitment to each other and started their lives together.

They married and settled in Orion, Indiana, They got engineering jobs nearby, were able to purchase a small farm which was close to Jim's family. They were together and they were very happy. Yet, with all the joy in their lives, Elena did miss her parents. They were so important to her, and she longed for them to be close by and to share her and Jim's lives together. Dispute annual trips to Italy, it became so much harder to leave her parents each time. Moreover, a new chapter of life was beginning for Elena and Jim. They were having their first child.

Their beautiful daughter was born and named Sarah after her grandmother Sarafina. When they returned to Italy after her birth, her new grandparents were delighted. They quickly loved and adored her and the Famiglia had a wonderful visit. Sadly, the time for the family to leave came all too soon. The departure was agonizing and everyone wished it didn't have to happen.

Understandably, the time between the visits had become longer and traveling was difficult and expensive. Elena and Jim wondered if it was time for some kind of change. Could they convince Giacomo and Sarafina to consider emigrating to America? For years the couple had described the beauty of southern Indiana and had invited Elena's parents to come. But Giacomo and Sarafina could not be persuaded, despite their sadness at missing their wonderful children. The prospect of leaving Italy was just too overwhelming.

The birth of a second grandchild, named James after his father and grandfather, was to become a life-changing event. After meeting him on the family's next trip and seeing their Familia again, Sarafina and Giacomo quickly bonded to their precious grandson. Sadly, when they had to say goodbye, the grandparents, now Noni and Grampa, could no longer bear the separation. They decided it was time to think about going to America and to make a new home there. They excitedly told Elena and Jim. The couple began construction for a small farmhouse on their property. They designed it to be similar to the Italian home of Elena's parents. Time passed slowly it seemed, but soon all was ready for the parents to leave their beloved Italy. The Spangos were coming to America. It could not be a happier time.

Elena, Jim, and the children traveled to the nearby international to greet the newcomers. Love, joy, and excitement filled the terminal as each family waited eagerly for their loved ones to walk up the jetway. Groups of people came into the terminal and finally Sarafina and Giacomo were spotted. Each was carrying a very worn suitcase, and looked both elated and exhausted. They were two small dark figures, slowly coming into the terminal. They certainly stood out from the other passengers. Giacomo was also carrying an old brown blanket roll, which he seemed to hold on to with great concern. Elena surmised that her parents must have been worried about being cold on the plane!

For just a moment Elena experienced a pang of anxiety. She realized how difficult this must have been for her parents. They had literally stepped out of one country for a new one. Was this going to be too much for them? Could they make the transition? Was it after all, the right decision? Was this going to work out for her precious parents? Time would have to be the answer.

And so for these two resilient and adaptable immigrants, there was no problem! They adjusted easily and quickly, loved being so close to their family, and knew they had made the right decision. They got right to work, making the house a home, working the small farm, and caring for a few farm animals. The gardens became lush, and the milk from the cow and goats was quickly turned into fresh cheese.

The couple was loving their new country. Elena, Jim, and the children radiated in the love from her parents. They had many meals together. They invited Jim's family and many friends for wonderful dinners. Sarafina made pasta and bread, Giacomo roasted vegetables and meat in an outdoor stove. They baked pizza in a wood fired oven. They created tantalizing pastries

All was going so well. This was the right and best decision for Sarafina and Giacomo to be in this new country. It was a dream coming true. Any fears Elena had for her parents disappeared. No chance they would go back to Italy. All was so good.

That is until one autumn day when her parents asked to speak to Elena and Jim at their home. Was something wrong? Were her parents unhappy? Elena felt a surge of anxiety. Was everything going to change? Jim and Elena both displayed their concern on worried faces. Seeing this, Giacomo quickly reassured them. Nothing was wrong. They were very happy, but they did want to do something a little more with their lives! They said they loved the farm, loved raising and cooking fresh foods, loved having people to share their blessings. In short, they wanted to open a restaurant in Orion!

Surprise and relief was immediate. Open a restaurant, in Orion? Did they know how much work this would be? Did they know how much money it would cost? Elena was confident that her parents had enough to live on, but where would they get that kind of money for a restaurant?

Sarafina and Giacomo both laughed a little. They knew what the problems would be, but still they were confident. And they had the money!

Giacomo asked if they remembered the old brown blanket roll they had brought on the plane. He explained that it seemed the safest way to carry their money. They had converted all their euros into dollars and carefully tucked them into the rolls is the blanket. They had the money and simply wanted their children's blessing for the venture.

Is it necessary to detail the success of their venture? Did they open a restaurant, did people come to enjoy their wonderful food? Was this another dream come true in a new country? Well, the next time you are traveling in the Midwest and happen through Orion, Indiana, drive down the Main Street, and take a deep breath. You may smell pizza and bread baking in a wood fired oven. You may smell spaghetti sauce bubbling, and vegetables and sausage roasting and sending out amazing aromas. You may pass a quaint and inviting place with a sign out front that says: *Sarafina and Giacomo's Eyetalian Home Cooking: The Best in the New Country.*

Compiled By: Roy L. Wachter

## BINOCULARS
Roy L. Wachter

706 Euclid Ave., Orion, Indiana

Yesterday was the last day of school before summer break and also my birthday. I'm ten years old now and can't wait until I'm 16 and can get my driver's license. Almost every week I ride my bike across town to look in the car lots and imagine driving one of the sleek Dodge Chargers or perhaps a Mustang. I imagine that my car will be red with white interior. My parents got me a pair of binoculars for my birthday. The binoculars are very powerful. My sister Trudy is jealous. That makes me happy since Trudy is my folk's favorite and usually gets all the really neat stuff. I never realized how much those binoculars would affect my life.

    Yesterday after the cake and ice cream and the traditional singing of Happy Birthday, I started to explore the neighborhood around Euclid Ave. Standing in the street I could see all the way to the park at the east end of Euclid. By adjusting the focus I could actually see children on the swings and slide. I saw one boy push a little girl off a riding toy and take her place. She ran crying to her mother and shortly the boy was removed and given a harsh talking to. The smile on the girl's face reminded me of similar scenes when Trudy got my mother to take her side.

    I turned to view the backyard of the best looking girl in the 4th, will be the 5$^{th}$, grade next fall. I've always had a crush on Juliana and sometimes I think she likes me too. Her folks have a pool in their backyard and I was hoping to see Juliana in a swim suit. It was not meant to be because the Johnsons had an eight foot tall wooden fence around the perimeter of their yard; in fact, most other backyards in our subdivision had similar fences. I realized I needed to look out of my bedroom window from the second story if I were to see anything in our neighbor's backyards.

From the higher vantage point of my second story window I could see Mr. Green baste steak on his grill, Mrs. Geardellie cut some roses from her garden and put them in a vase to carry into her house, and two boys light firecrackers and toss them into the lawn. I continued to snoop on my neighbors even after dark. The days were getting longer and the nights shorter and I didn't have any school the next day. I barely slept that night. My 10th birthday was exhausting.

I slept late the next morning. But when I awoke, I immediately grabbed my binoculars to see if anything interesting was happening in our neighborhood. I wanted to share my new found adventure with my two best friends, Isaac Benjamin Rosenthal and Daylin Allen Foster. Hanging the binoculars by the strap around my neck I got my bike out of the garage and rode to Daylin's house about a half mile down Euclid.

Daylin was in his driveway shooting baskets. I watched him sink five in a row from about 20 feet away. Daylin was probably the best athlete in the 5th grade. He could run and jump and throw and catch better than anyone else I'd ever seen. As he threw the basketball to me, he said, "What's up Charlie? What's your plan for today?" He called be Charlie because my name is Charles Dewayne McCall.

I took the binoculars from around my neck and handed them to Daylin, "Here try my birthday present; I think you'll like it."

Daylin took the binoculars and looked around, "Wow, these are powerful! How can you find what you want to see?"

I showed Daylin how to adjust the zoom on the binoculars and handed them back. "You have to see the big picture then carefully zero in on smaller objects."

After Daylin got the hang of the binoculars, he and I rode our bikes to Isaac's house. Isaac lived just across Euclid and down three houses from my house. When we entered Isaac's house, he was playing some type of video game that I didn't recognize. Despite the fact that binoculars are old technology, Isaac was impressed with the possibilities they presented.

We rode to my house and for the next couple of hours we took turns viewing from my second story window until Isaac said, "We need to be higher so we can see over all the privacy fences." He followed this remark with a detailed explanation of how a drone would work much better. He seemed to know a lot about drones.

"How about climbing high up in a tree?" Daylin suggested.

Isaac smiled as his enthusiasm grew, "How about the attic window at my house? It's higher than two stories."

Getting into Isaac's attic was difficult. We needed to move some clothing out of a closet in the hallway then push up a hinged lid. There was a small window. However, it was almost impossible to see thru the fly specked glass and maze of spider-webs. We could see more details from this greater height, but the summer-sun made the cramped space very hot and uncomfortable. We quickly abandoned the attic.

The only tall tree was not in my yard but in our neighbors. It grew in the corner of the lot and close to our property. Each summer, we have enjoyed the shade it throws onto our lawn: we sort of think of it as our tree. Climbing that tree would require getting over the fence between us and the Millers.

Being the super athlete he was, Daylin ran to the fence, jumped to catch the top of the eight foot high fence, pulled himself up to stand on the top of the fence then reached up to grab a large branch nearest to us. He then climbed higher into the thick foliage.

"Come on up guys; the view is great from here!"

Isaac and I looked at each other in amazement, "No way can we do what you just did," I exclaimed.

Isaac seemed to ponder the situation for a couple of minutes then added, "If we could use a ladder to get to top of the fence, perhaps we could reach the branches from there?"

Several hours later, we had secured two long ropes from the lower branches of the tree to the top of the ladder that leaned against the fence. The ropes could be used like two hand rails on the side of stairs. Several shorter strands of rope were tied between the two longer ropes to form what looked like a rope ladder. Isaac, who wasn't well-coordinated, had no difficulty climbing into the tree.

Later that day, we nailed and tied some boards in place to make small but comfortable seats in the tree. We referred to the three seats in the tree as our tree house. We were concerned that our neighbor would see us and object until I realized the family was on a vacation. I still worried about my parent's reaction to our project. I especially worried that my sister Trudy would discover what we were doing and seize the opportunity to once again bring discredit to me and favor to her.

We saw several things that we wish we hadn't. Several houses down Euclid, one neighbor had a large vegetable garden. We saw both the man and his wife tend the garden. Then one day after we saw the couple drive away, another neighbor squeezed between two slats in the old fence and picked several vegetables from the garden. He pushed the vegetables back out through the broken fence before he squeezed out himself. None of us knew the names of either neighbor.

I asked, "Did we just see him steal from the garden?"

"I think so," agreed Daylin.

Isaac added, "Should we report what we saw to anyone?"

After some discussion we decided not to report what we had seen.

We saw a bicycle that we heard was stolen parked on the paved patio behind the house. Had our neighbors found the bike or had they lied about it being stolen? A pool party several doors away seemed to be a little too wild. We thought we saw some teenagers smoke some marijuana.

"I feel like we're investigators. Perhaps we can get a job working for the police." Isaac said.

"We could call ourselves the Euclid Street Investigators and advertise to help folks find stolen stuff." Daylin added.

I suggested, "Let's use our names for the name of our investigative service."

"How about the Daylin, Isaac, and Charles Investigative Service?" replied Daylin?

Isaac said, "I kind of like the Isaac, Daylin and Charles Investigators."

We sorted through several variations for our team's name, until we decided on Charles, Isaac, and Allen Investigative Service. Daylen's middle name is Allen. With that name we could call ourselves the CIA Investigators. Each time we used our name we smiled about our cleverness.

In late afternoon, just before my parents were to arrive home, I was careful to untie the ropes from the top of the ladder and retie them to the top of the fence. I would then lay the ladder behind some bushes so Trudy or my parents wouldn't notice. Most evenings Isaac and Daylin were with their own families and I manned the lookout tree house alone. After dark I would sneak out of the house to reestablish my post in the tree house.

One day we noticed a neighbor carry a round flat bale of hay into his yard and place in on a special stand to set up a target. He placed a large paper target on the bale and began to shoot arrows from his bow. At first he rarely hit the target and almost launched one arrow over his privacy fence into his neighbor's yard. However after a few hours of practice, he began hitting the bull's eye on the target. I became alarmed when he hung a photo of a woman, perhaps his boss or wife, in the center and smiled each time he sunk an arrow in her face.

Our house is at 706 Euclid and two houses away at 710 Euclid, beautiful flower-beds surround the entire yard just inside the fence.

My mother told me the couple that lived there were the McDonalds. She thought his name was Eugene and her name Linda, but she wasn't sure.

On most days I saw Mrs. McDonald working in her flower garden; Mr. McDonald never helped. One morning a new flower garden appeared in the middle of their yard and Mr. McDonald was now the gardener. Several days passed and I failed to see Mrs. McDonald again. When I asked, my mother, she thought Mrs. McDonald was away visiting her ailing sister in New Jersey.

From the tree house I watched Mr. McDonald unload bags of mulch and fertilizer and a variety of flowers in disposable pots. When I failed to see bags of top soil, I became curious. Where did the large pile of soil that formed the flower garden in the middle of the yard come from? With my powerful binoculars I could examine the soil in the new bed and discovered that it had small bits of roots and mulch in it. It definitely wasn't good top soil. He hadn't taken a delivery of soil onto his driveway like others often do. Since the new flower bed seemed to appear suddenly one morning, Mr. McDonald must have built in in the dark. Why would he work in the dark?

When I revealed my concerns to the other members of our CIA investigative team, we began to formulate a scenario.

I said, "I Think he killed his wife and buried her in the new flowerbed in the middle of the yard."

Isaac, "If he laid her body in the middle of the yard, then where did he get the soil to cover her?"

Daylin said, "He could dig soil from the other beds and use that."

I thought for a minute then added, "So her body lay in the middle of the yard while he moved shovel after shovel to cover her. I believe that would take more time than he would want her body to be exposed for his neighbors to see, even in the dark."

"What if Mr. McDonald dug a large hole in the existing flowerbed and piled the soil in the middle of the yard, then quickly carried his wife out into the yard and dropped her in the hole in the old flowerbed then quickly covered her," Isaac added.

"That would explain why the pile of soil in the new flowerbed has some roots and mulch in it." I said.

"Also, why did he replace some flowers in the old bed?" Daylin asked.

"And how to prove any of this?" I asked.

Isaac smiled, "We need to get into McDonald's backyard."

Isaac is amazing; he seems unafraid. Daylin is strong and athletic, Isaac is willing to take risks, and me, well, I'm a curious kid with binoculars.

Isaac hid behind a large trash-can beside the garage until Mr. McDonald came home from work. Isaac's timing was perfect; just as Mr. McDonald punched the numbers into his digital garage door opener, Isaac appeared to see and memorize the numbers. Then to distract Mr. McDonald from realizing what had just occurred, Isaac pretend to be a mentally handicapped boy who was visiting a friend in the neighborhood. He asked for directions to Daylin's house, thanked Mr. McDonald and wandered down the street.

Back at CIA headquarters in our tree house we discussed our possibilities. Daylin was cautious, "I don't think we should break into the garage then move through the house to get into the backyard. I'm sure that's illegal. Count me out."

"You're right; there must be another way," I added.

Isaac used his dad's battery powered drill and a Phillips bit to back out the screws holding one of the vertical slats of the fence around

Mr. McDonald's yard. Daylin and I took turns using the binoculars to watch Isaac as he pushed his small dog, Ginger, through the recently created hole in the fence then squeezed through himself.

As we watched from our tree, Isaac used a broom handle to probe into the mound of the new flower bed and the newly disturbed soil in the existing bed. We thought Ginger might smell a decaying body and start to dig. To our disappointment Ginger only sniffed and sniffed and then peed on what looked like a prize rosebush.

Back at CIA headquarters in our tree house, we heard Isaac's report. "I could tell that most of soil in the older flower bed was still firm. Only the newly planted portion was loose and somewhat crumbly. The entire mound of the new bed in the middle of the yard was still loose."

"Did your broom handle hit anything like a body?" Daylin asked.

"No!" I said, "I'm still confident that Mr. McDonald killed his wife and buried her in the yard."

"Me too." echoed the other two investigators.

"What should we do now?" I asked. "Should we go to the police or tell our folks."

Daylin stroked is chin and added, "Guys, we have been snooping on our neighbors. I don't think the police or our parents will appreciate that."

"And I be can arrested for trespassing when I crawled into Mr. McDonald's backyard."

"Let's meet again tomorrow and formulate another plan." I said.

Since it was nearing the supper hour and my parents would be home soon, we decided to end our meeting. Isaac rode west to his house and Daylin went east to his house.

I was placing the ladder in its usual hiding place, when Daylin came running into the yard yelling, "Guess what I just saw?"

I responded, "Daylin, settle down and just tell me."

"I just saw Mrs. McDonald pull into her driveway."

Once we called Isaac and he returned, the three of us sat on chairs on our patio to discuss our options. We realized that this meeting might be the final meeting of the CIA investigators.

I could see the disappointment on Isaac's and Daylin's faces. I know I felt like throwing my binoculars over the fence into my neighbor's pool. "I guess the CIA's first and maybe our last murder case will go unsolved!"

"Are we going to disband the CIA Investigative Service?" asked Daylin.

Suddenly Isaac jumped up out of his chair and exclaimed, "But do we really know what Mrs. McDonald looks like? Perhaps the woman you saw was his mistress or accomplice."

As our renewed enthusiasm grew, we gave high fives and I exclaimed, "The CIA Investigators are back in service!"

## VINCENT PRICE, RABBIT EARS, AND SNOW BUNNIES
Kathi Lengacher

### 207 Sycamore Street, Orion, Indiana

I was twelve years old when we toured the two-story house that would become our new home. A German merchant with the last name of Frank built the ten-room structure in 1867 for his family. That's about all the history that we know about it, besides the fact that his store had been at the corner of 8th and Main, here in Orion, and the building still stands to this day.

Mom carried my baby brother on our home tour while my younger sister and I followed behind the adults. We started down the spacious front hall. I recall the hall was wallpapered in green toile and the ornate cherry wooden banister captured my attention to the right. It seemed tall and lead to – who knows where.

"Now were does this lead too?" My mother asked the homeowner who was selling the property.

We stood at the far end of the entrance hall facing an outwardly curved wall. The curve started from the door to our left and ended at the door to our nose. Barely passed the front door and we were lost. The wooden door in front of us was locked. A door stood open to the right. There was another door inside that door facing left, and also a smaller door under the stairs was closed. We were befuddled by the enormity of the place and led by the homeowner to the left, under a glass transom.

"This is the formal dining room."

Wow I thought, still young enough to be entranced with Walt Disney princesses and castles, or at least Victorian mansions with a dash of grace. It was pretty with a chandelier hanging over a large table. There were two tall windows covered with wooden shutters, and a built-in cupboard in a corner. Behind us, through two formal sliding doors, was the living room. It was beautiful with a walnut fireplace mantle and original green tiles in excellent condition. Wooden beams drew the eye up to an eleven-foot ceiling. The bayed out window, large enough to walk into, was also covered with wooden shutters.

I had never seen anything like it before or a house so large. We had come from a home the size of a small apartment.

So, we were lost. Only as far as the dining room. A wall behind us curved inward. Yes, the backside of the curve from in the hall. There was a door at the end of the curve, locked, and a small opening that led to…

"Here are the basement stairs," the homeowner announced as we walked further to the back of the house. "The backstairs are above it but they were walled off when the house was turned into apartments in the 1940s. They end in the breakfast room."

Breakfast room? What does one do with a breakfast room when you only eat cereal in a hurry before rushing off to school?

Through a small hall we entered the spacious kitchen.

"The cabinets are original," the homeowner said.

"A yellow kitchen," mom remarked. "I like it."

I just saw big and old and wondered how my life would change.

We moved into the monstrous abode soon after the tour.

I quickly became accustomed to my room facing the front of the house. I suddenly had all the space in the world and no longer had to share a room with my sister and baby brother. I had a fireplace that didn't work and a five-bulb chandelier, pretty rose-colored wallpaper with matching velvet curtains and creamy lace sheers. I was a princess in her castle keep, with fanciful ideas of creativity, soon to be replaced with teenaged dreams.

The house was a blast. Mom decorated it quite Victorian, while my sister and I ran and played and our baby brother learned to scoot up and down the twenty-tread staircase. Oh, how that sounds so dangerous today.

The downstairs library was an interesting room. Our grandparents gave us quite a collection of reading material to put in the library, along with dad's growing collection of Readers Digest books. The shelves filled up from great-grandmother's schoolhouse readers. Also, with encyclopedias to works of literary fiction that lined a few shelves. My family held nearly first edition copies of a few classics from the late 1800s through the 1920s and '30s. The shelves were constructed from the bay window to the ceiling and around the next wall to the front window.

And so I read, and read, and studied. I learned about the Rosicrucian Library, the secrets of the Great Pyramid of Cheops, Atlantis and Lemuria. I read Hawthorne, Du Maurier, Twain and Dickens, and the works of Guy De Maupassant – from a 1903 first edition. We treasured the book about the sinking of the Titanic, which is currently in my sister's possession and under lock and key. The story was shocking and the book held pictures of a horrific nature. I also read short stories from a collection of great authors in a series of ten books – circa 1920, and always with a dictionary beside me for big words that I failed to understand.

"Whoop, whoop!" my sister and I sang loudly out an opened window. It was the fall of the year but still warm enough for short sleeves.

We waited and sure enough we faintly heard, "Whoop, whoop!" sang to us in return, and then we saw a bouncing young female with long blonde hair.

"Whoop, whoop, let's all chant," we sang like the Michael Zager band.

"It's the weekend! Can you come over and watch Tales of Terror with us?" my sister yelled to her friend.

"Yeah, I'll be over."

"It's Vincent Price and The Raven."

"Oh, cool."

Our parents were gone for the evening and we lived next to a flower shop. What kind of trouble could three teenage girls get into? Ha!

"Nevermore – nevermore," the voice on the television moaned in deep despair as it recited Edgar Allen Poe's dark poem of death and insanity.

And then there was a commercial. I don't know where I went or how I missed it… but in through the kitchen door my sister and her friend came frolicking as two wild flower children. They flung dead flower petals all over the floor leading into the living room, proceeding to make a total mess of the area with flowers in their hair, on the coffee table, and on the television…

"Here's to Leah'nore! Nevermore! Nevermore!"

"What are you guys doing?" I shrieked.

"We're bringing flowers to the dead Leah'nore."

"That's Lenore," I corrected them.

"Leah'nore," they both moaned in their best zombie voice.

"Well, I'm not cleaning up this mess. You guys do it before mom and dad get home or you're in big trouble."

The mess got cleaned up and our parents never knew that the living room floor was nearly covered, wall to wall, in dead flower petals. Well, for several years they didn't know.

And so as a teenager I began to write. The writing wasn't very good, but I sat up in my rose-colored room listening to music by the Osmond Brothers and creating stories of magic, or else something along the lines of a Starsky and Hutch episode or Magnum P.I. Creativity filled the void in my soul. It was something I had to do or go completely mad.

I don't think it had anything to do with the ghosts in the house. Yes, ghosts. Or for those non-believers of such things. The passionate creativity of my mind needed to be addressed for mere survival!

The attic stairs stood ominously outside my door to the right in the hallway. The place where I always felt the ghost resided. That is, when he wasn't in the library. We all felt a sense of uneasiness in the library, and the cat refused to go in there too. Dead people had been laid out for viewing in that room in the old days, and we even found a headstone in the backyard. Oh, and not to mention that a woman died of starvation in my room back during the Second World War. I was never scared though because she went to heaven. The coast was clear.

And so the white door to the attic staircase was always closed, but I had climbed up the steps before, with dad, and knew what to expect. The ascending steps, considered floating as they secured directly into the wall, were creaky and narrow, and being boxed in by a wall you never knew you were actually 13 to 25 feet above the ground. But in the back of my mind I knew one slip or break through the wood and there was no return. You were doomed to fall to the main staircase below. And get laid out in the library like Leah'nore. Nevermore.

The attic was dark and unfinished. In the center of the space was another staircase to the roof.

"Hey, sis, you want to sunbathe on the roof?" I asked one hot summer day.

"Do you think we'll get in trouble?"

"Nope, dad's not home. I can do it. I'll open the attic roof door. It's kind of heavy but we can do it."

"But dad says walking on the roof makes it leak."

"So. He walks on it and we don't weigh as much as him."

We set our towels on the roof on what could only be considered a widow's walk without the railing. It was raised and square. And the view? It was awesome. You could see all of downtown and the courthouse, and more. We only did that once and thankfully did not get caught.

"Hippty hop hop. Hippty hop hop. Easter's on its way!" My sister and her friend sang while stomping up the stairs and then hopping into her room, which was to the right and immediately off the landing.

They turned the music up loud filling the house, and proceeded to dance like madmen.

"Stop stomping the floor," dad bellowed from the first floor. "You're making the ceiling plaster fall in the junk room!"

Sis's room was above the junk room. The only room where plaster seemed to fall, liberally as time went on and as we got older. The house was old. A money pit. The windows were not completely weather proofed and eventually the roof had to be replaced.

But the holidays, Christmas especially, were to be treasured. The stockings were hung by the chimney with care and by mom. And we always had a real tree decorated in the library's bay window. It filled the bay perfectly and smelled delicious. I can still recall the old-fashioned light strands that heated up and warmed the oils of the tree creating an unmistakable scent that is lost today.

But I digress.

The dancing hopsters in my sister's room continued dancing even after dad yelled. I came around the corner of our adjoining rooms and stopped. On their heads were headbands with bright glittery rabbit ears. There was a spiraled spring between the headband and rabbit ears, and the girls looked adorable standing next to the white canopy bed.

"Oh cute," I remarked.

"We skipped down Main Street with these on our heads," one of them explained. "Everybody looked at us and cars honked too."

Okay, I had to laugh hysterically. I could just visualize those two doing that.

The winter of 1979. Who can forget the deep snow?

We lived on a hill, perfect for sledding into the side street. The street was safe and rarely used. We spent hours playing in the snow before coming inside for hot chocolate. Our brother too.

We lived across the street from a business that needed traffic cones on occasion, not to mention our street was the emergency snow route.

Hmm, traffic cones and emergency snow route? Oh, yes, those two did it! Sis and her friend, I'm not sure who was the biggest conspirator, put the cones out in the snow-covered street where even emergency vehicles were afraid to go through the barricade. I have reminded them of this occasionally through the years.

The tornado of 1990 went through town and tore things up pretty bad. I was home with mom as we hunkered down under the main staircase. We took turns opening the door and yelling for the Siamese cat to 'get in here.' She survived just fine along with the Cockatiel bird caged in the breakfast room.

But during the tornado and hiding under the stairs, mom and I could hear the windows breaking and we knew the moment the air conditioner ripped from the front window. We didn't realize the brick front porch was being ripped away due to the roar of the storm, or that the old trees were all being ripped from the ground. The roof also raised and came back down, two inches from where it should had been originally. The outer wall between my sister's room and mine crinkled inward a few inches due to the roof heaving. What mom and I realized for certain in the middle of all the action was that the walls seemed to bow in and out, slowly as if they were breathing from a set of lungs. Insulation crept through the hallway, polluting the air. The serge of the storm was frightening and exhilarating all at the same time. The sheer energy and power of the tornado was – there is no word to describe the raw force of Mother Nature, condemning any sense of status quo and changing our lives forever.

The house supported my parents for a few more months before a scrap crew bought it out and dismantled the woodwork, fixtures, and the cherry staircase. I heard the pieces went to Indianapolis to be sold as antique restoration for other homes. My sister, her husband and I saw the house a few days before it was torn down. We stood in the grass below our bedroom windows recalling how we knocked on the wall between our headboards and talked until we fell asleep.

As I stood outside the house and looked around the property it was sad. We recalled finding the antique brick pathway under the lawn, and the tiny miniature rose bush, peachy-pink in color, that our brother killed by running his toy cars around it. And Sir Flip-flop, our basset hound lived in the yard until we gave him to an aunt who lived in the country.

I really didn't want to be there the day they tore the house down. Rumor has it the demolition team shoved everything into the basement cavity and let it burn.

However our ghost, who we called Mr. Frank, had the last laugh in the end. A new business constructed their building on the site where our house had been. Early on it suffered an accident. We learned that soon after the brick structure was finished, late one night the glass on the front door blew out – from within. Glass lay shattered in dozens of pieces on the front sidewalk. No one ever figured out how it happened. But we know. It was probably his last hurrah as he moved on to greener, or else sky-blue pastures.

Although the house is long gone, funny thing is, it's still with us. In pictures and in our dreams. I can still see creaky floorboards and certain aspects as vividly as if it were yesterday. There is an antique musk rose bush in my current backyard that I cultivated from the yard of the old house. The shrub flourishes in abundance.

And. The old antique books from the library room, the ones that really mattered, are with me and sitting on my bookshelf. Forevermore. Forevermore.

# I'M MY BROTHERS KEEPER
## C. B. Buckley

The Orion basketball players thumped down on benches gasping for breath. Towels swiped perspiration from faces after another grueling practice. Coach Bradley rolled his tongue across his teeth. "It has been brought to my attention that you want the Correctional Center fellows removed from our schedule. Why is that?"

Faces disappeared into towels, except one. "Well, coach, it's this way. last year the Correctional boys came into our gym with no fans, no cheerleaders, and everybody yelled for us. Our guys don't want to ever play under those conditions again. Please take them off our schedule," pleaded Roy, the team's captain known for his gritty, blue-collar rebounding.

"Well, I wasn't expecting that! Gentlemen, it's too late to take them off of our schedule! You know, legal-binding contracts have been signed between the parties. We must play them," explained Tom Bradley, the successful basketball coach who now spoke like a Houston lawyer.

Jerome looked up from his colorful sneakers. "I can't believe that little inmate had the audacity to elbow me in the face last year!"

"I can't believe that you, Jerome, of all the players on this team, would have a pity party because you caught one in the mouth. You know that happens in nearly every one of our basketball games," snorted Coach Bradley.

"I know, coach, but this was the first time that I was hit in the mouth and pick-pocketed at the same time, laughed Jerome.

"Jerome, you've come a long way, big guy. It wasn't too long ago you had a pouting party every time I gave you advice," admonished Coach Bradley," but now you know how to make all of us laugh."

"Floyd, the respected senior, suggested, "Since we have to play those guys again, let's make the playing field level."

Coach Bradley took a slug of water from his nifty water bottle. "Where are you going with this?"

"I have an idea. This year let's have some of our fans and our cheerleaders yell for the correctional team," said Floyd.

Jerome throws down his towel. "Are you out of your mind? Why should those criminals get any kind of support? You want people to yell and support those who commit crimes! What kind of message does that send out to the little kids?"

Tyrone, the star athlete, took personal offense. "I guess you believe that a person cannot change, but that's wrong. A person can become a good citizen after making a mistake."

Jerome reacted, "You can't change a leopard's spots! You're talking about the exception to the rule! Most criminals are criminals forever! What do you think, coach?"

Coach Bradley looked down at his clip board. "Let's face it. Most coaches are 'change' agents."

Jerome asked, "What do you mean by 'change-agents'?"

"Jerome, I remember when you were a freshman. You had to make an important decision. Run the streets or play basketball? But you wisely decided to take the high road and become a good player. That change in your life didn't come cheap. It required much work and commitment. Basketball changed your life. You now had something to pin your pride on. You know that many young people are not born as criminals, but find themselves making bad decisions as teenagers. Often they follow others down the wrong path. They need change-agents to put them on the right track."

"Thanks, coach," muttered Jerome.

Floyd saw an opening. "That's what I was talking about. Everyone makes a mistake. I've certainly made my share. The only difference is some people get caught and serve time in prison.

Others luck by and never get caught."

Coach Bradley smiled. "Floyd, I'm glad that you didn't name anyone specifically. You may have stepped on some toes. But what causes a teenager to end up behind bars?"

Floyd takes a slug of water and releases, "My old man taught us from the get-go to choose our friends wisely."

"You're lucky to have a large pool of friends to choose from. I just had the cousins down on the West side. Those suckers hated whities, the po-lice, and especially those Uncle Toms who tried to better themselves," snorted Tyrone.

Sid, the black ninth-grader, liberated from the hood thanks to his basketball skills, rotated his neck in his hands to rid his never-ending neck pain. "My pal here, Tyrone, could've easily gone down that golden path as many of the blood have. You know, don't try to learn, don't try to earn, just sell drugs and be the big rich man."

Tyrone agreed. "If it weren't for Jackson at the Community Club for investing his time in me, I would probably be playing with the Correction Fellows. Yeah, I can just see me elbowing Jerome in the mouth and zipping out of here."

Jerome preferred to be a victim. "I was brought up with an alcoholic father who came home and beat the crap out of me and my mother. That didn't give me the right to steal and plunder and end up sitting behind bars."

Coach Bradley shook his head. "I never could figure out why two siblings who grew up with the same terrible circumstances end up in different places in life. One spends every day in prison while the other brother helps young people at the community center."

"You, coach, and Jackson intervened in my life at the right time as if you had been divinely sent," said Tyrone.

"Oh, no, I'm no saint." Coach Bradley had to hide behind his water bottle.

Sid saw his opening as he did so often before his drives to the basket. "If it were not for Jackson and Coach Bradley helping

Tyrone, I wouldn't be in this school where good grades are looked on in a favorable light. Tyrone paved the way for me and I'll always be grateful to him."

"Listen, little brother, you'll never be a Tyrone, but you could be something special your senior year if you work hard every day like Roy does."

Coach Bradley also saw his opening. "I think that we are all in agreement. If it had not been for someone entering our lives at the right time, then we could easily be playing for the Correctional team. I like the idea of treating those kids with some dignity because they just might need it now. Yes, Floyd, let's play them with half of our fans and cheerleaders yelling for them."

"Coach, I didn't think much of Floyd's ideas. He's known for some odd ones, but I think that this gesture of sportsmanship on our part is not a bad idea. I'm going to tell you fellows something, but I want it to stay here. I certainly do not want my father to hear about it. Two years ago on New Year's Eve I was winning in a poker game with friends my father would not approve of and fortunately did not know about. My other friends invited me to break-in to an elementary school and play basketball. I was winning in poker and decided not to go. The police got a tip from a neighbor and arrested my friends who all got 'breaking and entering' on their rap sheets. In fact, one of them played on the Correctional team last year and laughed when I got elbowed in the mouth. Yes, only through the grace of God, I could have played for the Correctional team too," confessed Jerome.

"Thanks, Jerome, for having the courage to tell us that incident. It will certainly stay here with this team. I'm proud of you guys wanting to take the high road and showing the highest in sportsmanship to a correctional team. I'll tell our athletic director about your desires. He'll be pleased because in this dog-eat-dog competitive atmosphere of basketball, it's indeed refreshing. You are dismissed after you shoot fifty free-throws. Good practice, guys!"

*(This story was based on a 2015 true story of a private school in Waco, Texas welcoming a surprised Correctional Team with their own cheerleaders and fans...score one for sportsmanship!)*

## BIG BIRD
### A.J. Gardner: 12-13-14

Big fat bird up on a limb
was told by his relatives,
"You'd better get slim.
Your heart won't put up with that
roll around your belly. It's already
shaking like a bowl full of jelly!

"But it's Christmas time and I can't resist that
chocolate-covered worm. I'd even eat a caramelized
cricket if I could just see him squirm.
Put some mint-covered ants in front of me,
and I'll leap into the air, chirping with glee."

And it's Christmas time with all
that junk food around.
And as for REDUCING,
I don't want to hear a sound."

"So just squeeze up to my big fat belly
and wish me Christmas cheer.
After all, Sweet Thing, this only happens
ONCE A YEAR!"

## RETURN TO ORION
Roy L. Wachter

I can't believe I'm going back to Orion, Indiana. It's been eight years since I left for college and my parents moved away one month later. I have many fond memories of Orion High School and I'm not really sure why I didn't come back sooner. I suppose since my parents moved to Madison just as I left for college, going home during breaks from class meant driving to Madison, not Orion. I could wait until our tenth year class reunion in two years but I'm at a crossroad in my life and I need to settle something now. I want to see Charlie, Dave, Brian and some of the other guys on the team. I hope some of them are still in town.

I shouldn't try to kid myself, I didn't return earlier because I was afraid to see Kathy Miller again. Our break-up was very painful and I didn't want to see her. Studying, working part time, and participating in fraternity activities kept my focus at Indiana University and off Kathy. The four years I spent in the Army after college didn't completely take my mind off Kathy. I was sure that I had moved on with my life despite losing the love of my life in Orion, but during the times I was alone I kept seeing her and wanting to talk to her, hug her, look into her beautiful hazel eyes, and run my hands through her auburn hair.

I can't get her out of my mind. I can't form another relationship with a woman because I keep comparing her to Kathy. I know she will have changed since we were 17. I imagine she lives in Orion; she seemed reluctant to leave eight years ago. She probably married that Gary West guy and they have a house full of kids. If that's what happened, I want to know for sure. I have to stop imagining I can come back to Orion and rekindle the fire we once shared. She won't even remember me. That's absurd; of course she'll remember; we shared a love that was meant to last a lifetime. How could things have gone so wrong? I guess we were just kids. After checking into the Holiday Inn Express, I drove around town to see what might have changed. There was a new Junior High School near the highway. A Chick-Fil-A and Hardees had been built near the exit off Barrow Street. A new asphalt track had replaced the old cinder track around the football field. Seeing the track and the football field brought back memories of football games and track meets. During high school I had played football, basketball, and ran track. I spent many, many hours either practicing or competing. Probably too many!

I drove through the old neighborhoods, past Brian's house and Martha's house. They looked pretty much like I remembered; however, Brian's had a different color siding. I felt melancholy as I stopped in front of 821 Oak St. where my parents, my brother and I had lived. Although it wasn't dilapidated, the house was in need of some tender loving care. My mother loved that house, her first and only new house, and I hoped she never would see it in disrepair.

I felt trepidation as I approached Kathy Miller's old house. I remember the address well, 103 Maple St. But there wasn't a house, only a weedy vacant lot with a for sale sign. Suddenly I remembered all the times I stood on the small porch and said goodnight to Kathy. Our first kiss and many of those that followed were shared right there on that porch. Seeing the porch and the entire house gone seemed to slam a door shut on a part of my memory that was vital to whom I am. I felt that all my joys and longings were somehow invalidated right at that moment. I wished I hadn't returned to Orion.

Whenever I feel frustrated or despondent I eat some comfort food. This was exactly one of those times. I headed to McDonalds adjacent to Chick-Fil-A. While enjoying a large vanilla milkshake, I looked around to see if I knew any of the customers from when I lived in Orion. I thought I recognized a girl from my class working behind the counter. I approached and asked, "Are you Angela; I've forgotten your last name?"

"Yes my name is Angela; it says so right here on my name tag."

"I feel foolish now. I'm not trying flirt with you. I use to live here and am trying to look up some old friends."

"Too bad."

"Too bad, I'm trying to find old friends."

"No, it's too bad you're not flirting with me. You're kind of cute."

I hadn't noticed Angela's eyes or hair until then.

"So are you."

"And who are you?" she asked.

I extended my hand and said, "I'm Jeff, Jeffery Brown. I graduated from Orion High eight years ago."

"I've been out for four years. My sister might have been in your class. Her name is Margret, Margret Winters. Do you remember her?"

"Was she a cheerleader?"

"That's her. Exactly who are you looking for? Maybe I can help."

"This girl lived on Maple Street. The house has been torn down. Her last name is, or was, Miller."

"I know exactly who you mean. It was a sad story. The house caught fire and was so damaged it had to torn down. The older couple moved to Dale where they had other relatives.

"That's her. I remember that her parents were older than most. I think they were actually her grandparents. Do you know if she still lives in Orion?"

"If fact, I do. She lives with her husband and children on the south side of town. I don't exactly know the address, but their house is near the end of the lane out by the water tower."

My heart sank with the mention of a husband and children. But I figured she would marry Gary West and live happily ever after. I still wanted to see her and talk. "Does she work out of the home or is she a full-time housewife?" I tried to mask my anguish when I asked. I must not have been successful.

"Are you OK Mister?"

"I'll survive."

"You can find her working at Bubba's Bar and Grill, She waits tables at noon."

I had difficulty getting my head around the image of Kathy waiting tables. I imagined Kathy would marry Gary West and live in a big house with many children. When Gary West came to town our senior year he seemed to have money and a bright future. He made good grades and was almost immediately popular. Although I didn't spend much time with Gary, I thought he was very likeable. I can still picture the shiny blue Mustang he drove. Most of the rest of us had to borrow our dad's car or had an older car.

I decided to go into Bubba's for a BLT sandwich for lunch. My plan was to observe Kathy from as far away as I could. I selected a table that was in the corner and being served by another waiter. I sat turned slightly so she might not recognize me before I was ready.

Immediately I recognized her Auburn hair. It wasn't as long and silky as I remembered. She had gained several pounds since high school. I guess having babies does that to some women.

During a break from the lunch crowd I approached Kathy as she stood at the counter restacking the menus. I stood slightly behind and to the side of her. "Kathy it's me, Jeff."

When she turned to face me, her face looked drawn and stressed. Her smile lacked the sparkle that I remembered. "Can I help you, sir?"

"You don't remember me do you?"

"Should I?"

I realized this woman wasn't the Kathy I had loved. "I'm sorry; I thought you were Kathy Miller."

"I'm Karen Garret, use to be Miller. I'm Kathy's younger sister. Who are you, again?"

"My name is Jeffery Brown; I use to date your sister."

"Now I remember. You guys were always together. Everyone thought you guys were the best looking couple in school. I sort of had a crush on you myself. I was sorry when you guys broke up."

"I'm sorry I didn't recognize you today. I didn't really notice you back in school."

"Yeah, you couldn't take your eyes off Kathy long enough to recognize the very attractive little sister who wished she were older." Karen laughed at her own humor.

Karen looked to table near the window, "Excuse me, I need to serve table number eight."

Once Karen returned, I asked, "Did Kathy marry Gary West and leave town?"

"Not really. A couple of months after you left for college there was talk of them getting married, then suddenly Gary West and his family moved out of town. Rumor was that Mr. West had to move to Texas to take another job in the oil industry. He worked for Halliburton, you know."

My heart leaped at hearing this news. "Did Kathy marry someone else? She wouldn't by chance still be in Orion, would she?"

"Yep, she lives in a small farm house at the north edge of town. No, she's not married."

I was sure Karen could hear my heart pounding inside my chest. "Can I see her? Do you think she wants to see me after all these years?"

Karen gave me a knowing smile and replied, "I know she would be glad to see you again. She often talks about the great times you two had together. I think she misses you."

"Where can I find her?"

"Well. Kathy has two jobs; she writes for the newspaper and works at the library." Karen glanced at her watch; "This time of day she would be at the library."

A new modern library sat on the corner of 4th and Main where the old Carnegie style library had been. The front entrance on 4th St. was made of glass. Even the two large doors of the entrance were made of glass. I had hoped to enter the library and stay out of view until I had seen Kathy from a distance. I was afraid that, being older, she had gained even more weight than her sister Karen. I was prepared for the worst.

Even before I pulled the doors open, I spotted Kathy standing behind the counter several feet ahead. I waved. She waved. I'm sure I had a silly grin as I approached. She stepped from behind the counter. When we met in the middle of the room, I extended my left hand, palm up. Kathy placed her right hand on mine. She extended her left hand and I covered it with my right. For several seconds we stood holding hands and grinned at each other. I'm sure Kathy could feel the pulse surging in my hands. Then I pulled her close and locked her in a bear hug lifting her off her feet.

By now, the other library employees and several patrons were staring at us. Kathy said, "Jeff, it's great to see you but I'm getting embarrassed. Let's go back in the office where we can talk."

Once we were out of public view in the office we embraced. "I've really missed you, Kathy. I think about you all the time." I kissed Kathy on her forehead and stroked her hair."

"I've missed you too Jeff."

After we pulled apart, I got a closer look at Kathy. Unlike her sister, Kathy hadn't gained much weight; her face was a little fuller, but not in an unattractive way. Actually I thought she looked better than when we were in high school. Her hair wasn't as long as before but the few highlights she had added made it more interesting. The three freckles, two small and one a little larger, on her nose reminded me why I had fallen in love with her.

Kathy's smile melted any reservations I had. She locked her still beautiful hazel eyes on mine and softly said, "I have to get back to work; can we finish this later?"

"When do you get off work?"

"My hours vary; since this is Tuesday, at 5 pm."

"I'll be here at 5 pm so we can get reacquainted. Better yet, I'll wait around and watch you work?"

"Don't be ridiculous, Jeff. I can't concentrate with you watching and I'd like to go home and shower before we meet again. How about dinner at the Great Wall? I think I remember that you liked Chinese food."

"Ok, it's a date. See you at your house at six pm. Oh; I guess I don't know where you live. I probably would have driven to the house where you lived in high school. Sorry about the fire. Sorry to hear your parents have passed." Kathy's expression cued me to conclude, "I think I'll shut up now."

Kathy gathered a piece of paper from the desk and drew a quick map to her house. "Take this and let me get back to work."

When she offered me the map, I grasped her hand holding the map and gently kissed the back of it.

As she pushed me out of the office and escorted me to the library door, Kathy muttered, "You haven't matured one bit over the last eight years"

As I drove away, I muttered to myself, "I can hardly believe my good fortune; I have a date with Kathy Miller, the prettiest girl in Orion High School. I laughed out loud when I realized how ridiculous that thought was; Kathy Miller has been out of high school for eight years. We both have matured and any relationship we might have now has to be different.

I decided to reconnoiter and locate Kathy's house before I returned to the motel. Her house was surrounded by a cornfield, bean field and another residence. The house was neat and attractive just like Kathy. Very nice, I thought.

After filling the jeep's tank, I ran it through a car wash. I took considerable time vacuuming the inside, especially the passenger seat where Kathy would sit. Back at the Holiday Inn Express I showered and washed my hair. I took an inordinate amount of time selecting my wardrobe. I settled for an open collared white shirt and dark trousers. I was almost as nervous as I was on our first date when we were sophomores in high school.

When I arrived at Kathy's house I had full intentions of walking up to her door, ringing her doorbell, escorting her to my jeep and holding the jeeps' door open. Before I rounded the front of the jeep, Kathy skipped down the drive to open the jeep's door herself. She hesitated to take the passenger seat. "Can I drive? I've always wanted to drive a jeep!"

"Kathy, you're still as independent as I remember. Sure, you can drive, but try not to roll the jeep; I'm really looking forward to Chinese for dinner. By the way, you look gorgeous.

And she did. Kathy had taken time to curl her auburn hair into loose curls that cascaded down to reach her chin. A small amount of eye shadow drew attention to her sparkling hazel eyes. And, as usual, those three freckles drew me in. I was thankful that she was driving. If I had been, Kathy would have been a major distraction.

Although the food was served buffet style, neither of us returned to replenish our plate. The food seemed to be a distraction from our conservation. I really love crab Rangoon, and sweet and sour chicken, but I didn't eat all I had taken. Our focus was on each other. Others in the restaurant seemed to disappear. We touched hands frequently. We smiled a lot. We laughed a lot. Once I did look around the room I noticed that all the customers were new. The owner was sternly looking at us. I glanced at the clock on the wall. "Kathy, we've been talking for almost two hours now; perhaps we should leave?"

"I would have you come to my house and continue our reminiscing but I need to get some sleep tonight. I have to be at the Orion Herald early tomorrow morning. I'll need to work some at home yet tonight. I need to get my notes in order; I have to turn in a major editorial about the local school board fight by 10 a.m. so it can go to press. Sorry about cutting our time together short."

I drove this time. I really wanted to kiss Kathy goodnight but once we stopped, she jumped from the jeep, waved goodbye and ran up the door. I yelled after her, "Can I see you tomorrow?"

"You bet," she yelled back.

The next day I took some lunch to Kathy at the newspaper. That was the first day of a pattern that would continue for the next two weeks. Many evenings we would sit on her front porch in wicker chairs and recall good memories from our youth.

"Remember how, after home games, we would meet at Arnolds with the rest of the team and share a burger, fries and a chocolate milkshake. I don't think anyone on the team knew we were holding hands under the table." Kathy smiled.

I had to tell my favorite part. "I remember the time you kicked off your shoe under the table and ran your foot up my leg. It was a good thing we were in public or…"

"Or what," she teased. We laughed and reached across the space between the chairs to hold hands.

One sunny afternoon when Kathy didn't have to work, we drove out to McDonald's lake. We stored all our clothing except our swim suits and sandals in the jeep and wadded into the lake. The swim to the floating dock in the middle of the lake was quite refreshing. We lay on the dock enjoying the warming rays of the sun.

"Kathy, do you remember all the afternoons we spent out here on this dock?'

"I sure do. I thought you were the most handsome boy in a bathing suit I had ever seen. You even swam smooth like a fish."

"I remember I couldn't take my eyes off the beautiful girl beside me. When we were sunbathing and I should have had my eyes shut, I keep staring at your beauty. Even today, I'm still staring and thinking and thinking."

About that time I realized I needed to change the subject. "Kathy, do you remember our first date, when we stood on your front porch and each time I started to kiss you goodnight another neighbor would turn on their houselights and come out into the street to walk to Dr. Nathan's house three doors down the street. I recall I just lost my nerve and shook you hand."

"I'd forgotten about that. You remember the next day we found out that a patient of Dr. Nathan's had died and he was very upset. Jeff, that wasn't exactly our first date. If you remember you stood me up on our first date."

"I remember that fiasco well. Mr. Queen our band director was leaving to go to another school. Many of our friends, including you, planned a going away party in the gym. Martha or Brian or one of the others asked if I wanted to contribute some money toward a gift for Mr. Queen. I didn't have much, but gave them a contribution and asked if I could attend the party since I had contributed to the gift. They said I was welcome to attend. Then a couple of days later you approached me in study-hall and asked if I wanted to contribute. I said I already had. You replied, "Do you want to be invited to attend the party by me?" Not realizing what you were asking, I agreed.

"The day of the party I spent 6th period helping you and some other band members set up tables and chairs for the party. All the time we were working side by side I wanted to ask you to the party but I knew how popular you were and was sure some other band member had already secured you for a date. I was humiliated when I entered the gym and your best friend came up to me and asked, "Why didn't you pick up Kathy?"

"Well I think I forgave you ten years ago."

Kathy touched her flat stomach and remarked, "I think I might be getting too much sun."

I placed one leg over Kathy and rolled over on top.

"What are you doing?"

"I'm blocking the sun so you won't burn!"

Kathy pushed me off into the lake and said, "I don't believe you. Maybe we should swim back to the jeep and go home. The swim will cool you off."

I took several hours to move the books out of Kathy's spare bedroom so I could move my stuff in. I couldn't believe how many books she had. We had agreed we could share more time if I didn't have to leave each evening. I kept my room at the Holiday Inn Express and on most mornings I ate breakfast there. I felt I might give folks the impression I was staying in the motel. I don't think I really fooled anyone. During the day when Kathy was working I often wondered around town and tried to visit with some people I remembered. Many of the folks would introduce me to others as Kathy Miller's boyfriend.

One afternoon Kathy let me watch her at work. She had about fifteen young boys and girls sitting on a large rug on the floor in the library. She sat on a low stool in the middle of the group and read a story to them. Kathy changed the inflection and tone of her voice to help animate the story. The boys and girls were enthralled by her. Their feelings of love and admiration for her were nothing compared to mine.

I had learned to cook a few simple things while I was in the Army but I was surprised how meaningful cooking with someone you love could be. We were able to share responsibilities and agree on the menu like we had lived together for years. We frequently touched and after sampling the taste of a dish we would kiss to share the taste

One evening when we were sitting on a park bench watching three Mallard ducks swim around the lake, I asked, "What happened to us Kathy? How did we lose what we had?"

Kathy looked as if she were about to cry. "I started to think you put sports ahead of me. You started to pull away; after we kissed you seemed to be in a hurry to leave."

"I pulled away because the smell and feel of you were causing me great physical and emotional stress. I know that you noticed the physical effect you had on me."

Kathy smiled. "I did notice the effect our hugging and kissing was having on you. I had similar feelings too."

I continued, "Our relationship was headed to another level. We were just seventeen years old. I had to slow things down. Then during the spring you started hanging out at Arnolds with some other kids from school. You seemed to enjoy the last few weeks of our senior year. I was happy for you. Your spending more time with the others took some pressure off our escalating relationship.

"I wasn't alarmed when you talked mostly with Gary West. I knew you enjoyed riding is his shiny Mustang with the others. Gary was new to Orion, very interesting and seemed like a nice guy. I liked him. He instantly became popular and had money to spend treating girls to movies and dinner. Several girls were very interested; he could have any girl he chose. I was sure that we had something special and nothing could change that but I was crushed when you agreed to go with Gary to our senior prom. Why did you do that?"

Although it has diminished over the last eight years, as I recalled the agony of that time in my life, I still felt the blow in my heart. My breathing became shallow and rapid. Looking through misty eyes, I could see the remorse in Kathy's eyes. She had tears running down her cheeks.

"I'm so very sorry. I know that was selfish of me," she moaned.

I took Kathy's hand and pulled her into an emotional hug. "I still love you, you know," I whispered.

"Kathy said, "I love you too" as she raised her head to share a long overdue kiss. I felt the fire of desire and the warmth of wholeness.

Kathy withdrew from our embrace. "Please let me explain; I want to explain."

"It's really not necessary."

Kathy continued, "I need to do this. There was a group of eight of us that started to hang out at Arnolds every day after school. They talked about driving to Cincinnati to Kings Island on Saturday after our prom on Friday evening. I really wanted to go. My grandparents and I never went anywhere. You had a big multiple team track meet on Saturday and didn't want to miss that. You also needed to get sleep on Friday night to prepare. In my mind, once again sports came first with you."

"I'm sorry things didn't work for us. How was your trip?"

"At first I thought I'd be fine and have a good time but as the day progressed I caught myself wanting to share a sight or experience with you. I knew I'd made a terrible mistake."

"Why didn't you tell me that the next week?"

"I'm not really sure; I think maybe I was ashamed of myself. You weren't exactly friendly if you remember."

"Well, Kathy, I was still hurting. I tried to get us back together by asking you to accompany me to Bloomington and attend IU. I thought if I could get you away from Gary, we could go back to being the couple we were. Why didn't you agree to leave Orion and go to College with me? I know your grades were good enough and you were eligible for financial aid"

"Well it wasn't because of Gary West, if that's what you think."

"Well, I did think that at the time, but I now know I was wrong."

"I'm not entirely sure why I won't go with you but I wasn't sure about us right at that time. Also I knew my attending college would cause some addition financial burden on my grandparents and they still had my younger sister to take care of. I guess I was afraid to leave Orion and the situation I was comfortable in. I intentionally was unfriendly saying no. I was afraid that you might reconsider and stay in Orion to be with me. I didn't want to limit your future because I was unsure of myself."

Kathy paused then asked, "Jeff can you ever love me again like you use to?"

"Kathy, the girl I once loved no longer exists. Neither of us are the same person we were eight years ago. We both have matured and are different people today. These two weeks we've spent getting to know each other has been wonderful. Sure we share a history, but I've fallen in love with a mature Kathy Miller. She is loving, kind, intriguing, beautiful, and sexually attractive. The woman I see standing before me is a new and improved version of the girl I knew in high school. So the answer is 'no.' I cannot love you like I did eight years ago but I can love you in a more meaningful way than the immature boy of eighteen ever could have."

We held each other for several minutes. I finally pulled away and said, "I have to leave Orion tomorrow and drive to Madison. My Dad called and said my Mother's Alzheimer's is getting worse and he needs me to help care for her. My brother lives in Colorado so I'm the only relative available.

"There is a second reason for me to travel to Madison. While in the Army, I made friends with a man named Bob Patton. He's no relation to General Patton. He and I plan to open a business in the old historical district of Madison called 'The Destination.' Bob called yesterday to say we needed to sign the final paperwork tomorrow.

Sorry I didn't tell you sooner but I was afraid to break the spell of our perfect week. Mainly 'The Destination' will be a book store/coffee shop combination. A local artist, baker and sculptor who live nearby have agreed to be vendors. The building is large and there will be plenty of space to display their craft. When I watched you read to the children in the library I realized the potential for learning sessions in the book store. It would be like a small library.

"Kathy, I want you go with me to start our adventure together. If you're concerned about housing, there's a three bedroom apartment above the store. It has two and a half bathrooms and a balcony that overlooks the Ohio River."

"Must you leave tomorrow?"

"Bob and I have to be at the bank to sign the final paperwork to finalize the deal. I need to be there at 10 a.m. tomorrow."

After what seemed to be an eternity of silence, Kathy replied, "Do you expect me to go with you tomorrow or will you be back in few days?'

"I was hoping you could go with me tomorrow, at least to see the property we will own."

Kathy said, "Listen to yourself. If we build a life together will you always decide important things without considering my views or wishes. Will you just order me around and drag me wherever you wander."

I was not prepared for Kathy's response. "I'm sorry if I seem to be moving too fast. I'm not used to considering what others think. I usually decide and accept the consequences. I really want to spend the rest of my life with you."

"If I agree to move to Madison, I'll be walking away from two jobs I really love. Also I own the house you have been sleeping in. It has furniture. I don't think I can go tomorrow. Can't we take things a little slower and wait and see how things progress?"

Without looking into Kathy's eyes, I said, "I need to go back to your house and pick up my things and move them into the motel. I'll be leaving from there early tomorrow morning." My tone was not friendly.

Only after we had driven to Kathy's house and she had helped load my jeep did either of us speak. I gently hugged her and said, "It seems we have acted out this scene before so I'll say goodbye again."

Kathy tried to discretely wipe away a tear as she said, "I guess this is goodbye then."

The Holiday Inn Express had advertised the comfort of their beds by guaranteeing a restful night's sleep. That night was anything but restful. I tried to watch TV to distract myself from the hurt I was feeling. I couldn't stop rehashing our conversation.

Kathy never really said she wouldn't go to Madison to live with me did she? Was I even thinking straight? Was I letting my hurt from eight years ago cloud my judgment? Was I just trying to hurt her like she had hurt me? How could I be so foolish? I love her and hate her at the same time. I know I need her in my life. She did say she loved me didn't she? That woman has the power to make me feel terrific one minute and terrible the next. I've really messed this thing up now. I don't see any way to erase the pain I must have caused by leaving the way I did. I'm so sorry for my behavior. I never should have returned to Orion. I'll never come back again.

Sometime in the wee hours of the morning I finally fell into an exhausted slept.

The next morning I still felt exhausted as I loaded the blankets and quilts I had purchased into the back seat of the jeep. They lay in an unorganized heap but I really didn't care. I returned to my room to gather my suitcases and computer then placed them in the storage compartment behind the second seat. I had filled the tank with gasoline the night before so I could get out of Orion as quickly as possible.

I tried to purge any thought of Kathy from my mind but must have failed because I drifted well below the posted speed limit. I looked into my rear-view mirror to see a large pickup truck tailgating my bumper. He was anxious to pass. He honked as he passed and sped away.

Again I glanced to the rear-view mirror to see if any other vehicles had been slowed by my inattention. I saw one of the blankets move! "What the..." I exclaimed. A second glance into the back seat revealed a small hand extending from beneath the pile of blankets.

Suddenly Kathy sat up and exclaimed, "Jeff don't you think you should turn around and go back to get some of my stuff. A girl needs stuff too, you know!"

# FILL MY CUP
## Wini Fagen Frances

"Sell it!" I shouted into the phone. "It means nothing to me. I'm no farmer." That's what I told the attorney who tracked me down using Google people search. He notified me Mom and Dad had both passed on, and I had inherited the forty-acre farm. The lawyer informed me I needed to return to the county to sign papers and decide what to do about the farm. So here I am, headed toward the old home place in the boonies outside my hometown of Orion for one last visit.

I'd been away for years, trying to make my mark upon the world. To be and do something important and memorable. What a joke. Who did I think I was anyway? What could I ever do to make myself a household name? I wasn't an inventor like the Wright brothers. No chance of me finding a cure for cancer like Jonas Salk who discovered the polio vaccine. I'm technologically challenged, so no new electronic inventions in my future. I could barely figure out how to take pictures and check email on my smart phone. Oh well, life goes on. But definitely not the way I'd planned.

Shifting into four-wheel drive, I turned onto the rutted, red clay dirt road for one last visit to the old home place. The dilapidated old barn looked unsafe as it leaned sideways. Chunks of mortar and broken bricks cluttered the ground near the chimney. As I parked in the back, I spied the overturned outhouse. Boy! That sure brings back memories.

Then I noticed the dried up pond. I figured the old abandoned coal mine I passed on the way had something to do with the missing water. Blasts at the mine probably changed the course of the underground water.

I climbed from my pickup and walked around the house. Mom always planted a huge garden on the left side of the house, close to the well. She used to tell me she planted it there so I wouldn't have to carry the water so far. A dented old bucket still hung from the hook. But the frayed rope looked like it would break if I unwound it and filled the bucket. I didn't see any water close to the top, so I fished my phone from my pocket. Using the flashlight on it, I shined the light to the bottom of the well. Crusty, dried mud greeted my eyes. Not one drop of water.

Staring into the bottom of the well I reminisced about my life. I felt like that old dried up well. Like the garden plants when I neglected them. Wilted. Shriveled. And dying. Without hope. Then I remembered how the plants sprang back to life when I watered them. They revived, bloomed and bore fruit. That gave me hope.

Dear Lord, I don't know why I turned my back on You and the Church. I'm just like the woman at the well we sang about when I was a young girl. I was seeking for things that could not satisfy instead of seeking You, Jesus. I thirst for the living water from the well that will never dry up. I ask You to fill my cup and my heart, Lord. Quench the thirsting of my soul. Fill me up and make me whole.

Tears trickled out the corner of my eyes as I continued praying. I'm one of millions who craved earthly fame and fortune, Lord. I tried to build my treasure on earth where moth and rust destroy, and thieves break in and steal. Forgive me, Lord. Help me build my treasure in heaven so I can spend eternity praising You.

I thirsted in the barren land of sin and shame and nothing satisfied me, Lord. But I'm turning back to You and the springs of living water You offer so freely. It doesn't matter that my name isn't well-known. It only matters that it is recorded in the Lamb's Book of Life. Thank you, Lord that my name is written down in glory.

Tears streamed down my cheeks. I wiped my eyes with my sleeve and scrambled back into my pickup. Maybe I won't sell the place after all. I could turn it into a refuge for troubled teens. I could build a new pond and drill a new well. As I bounced down the rutted dirt lane, I envisioned the sign over the entrance: "LIVING WATER RANCH."

## NOTES FROM THE OTHER SIDE OF THE CIRCULATION DESK
Erin Maley

Ruth Fuller had been a library clerk at the Orion Public Library for five years on Monday. She doubted if any of her colleagues remembered that her five-year anniversary was coming up. After six months, she'd felt as if she'd worked there forever, and she knew they felt it too. For there was something significantly similar about all the library employees. It took one to know one, and they held in common many peculiarities, silently noticing but rarely remarking. Ruth liked to think there was a hint of immortality about them, as if they already knew what the afterlife held and had voluntarily returned to the present merely to assist the human race to greater knowledge.

There were many things that Ruth loved about her job.

She loved tidying the shelves. She would run her hand along the books' spines, flattening them against the edge of the shelf until a uniform row presented itself. She rescued the books that had been thoughtlessly shoved behind the others, hidden from view, and returned them to their rightful Dewey order. She would search for books that had been buried among a section not their own, and took great satisfaction in putting them back in their place.

She loved helping patrons find the books they were searching for. She would research patiently until they either found their object, or were content to put in an order for an inter-library loan, borrowing the book they wanted from another library.

Yes, there were many things that Ruth loved, but her job never quite matched what others' presumed it to be. Her friend Olivia, nearest and dearest since they were both aged five, had recently passed her bar exam after years of studying law.

On one of their recent coffee dates, Olivia had expressed jealousy for Ruth's chosen profession.

"You basically just sit around and read novels all day, don't you? Come on, admit it!"

Ruth was accustomed to Olivia's teasing. "Yes, that's what I do. You read a lot too!"

"Some days, when I have a big case coming up, that's all I do. But it's not reading for pleasure, let me tell you!"

"It might be time to remind yourself that your salary is twice the size of mine, Liv," Ruth retorted drily.

Olivia sipped her coffee. "Yes, I suppose that's true," she admitted, momentarily quenched.

"But the people! The public you work with is nothing compared to the ones we have to deal with. My last client was a murderer. I had to make constant prison visits. I'm sure I'll get used to it, but believe me, it's nothing like the bookworms you consort with on a daily basis."

Ruth did not know what to say. She savored another drink of coffee and thought about her friend's words.

They came back to her on Monday, her five year work anniversary. The library had been open for less than five minutes. Ruth looked up to see an unfamiliar patron breezing through the atrium at high speed. Her voice matched her pace. Ruth had to listen carefully to keep up.

"Hi! Now, I'm in a big hurry so I need you to work fast, here. I'm looking for a book called The Coming Apocalypse. I KNOW you have it. It was super popular a couple of years ago. They made a movie of it. Can you just tell me who wrote it and I'll go look myself? I don't want to disturb you from your jobs!" She nodded pointedly towards the huge pile of library materials waiting to be checked in, that Ruth had slowly been working her way through.

"Of course," Ruth said. She searched the library's online catalog. She found the book's title, clicked on it, and sighed inwardly when confronted with the location: Lost. "I'm sorry, ma'am. That book appears to be lost."

The woman's mouth dropped open and she made an impatient motion with both hands. "What? But it was such a popular book! And a movie!"

"I know. Unfortunately, books like that often end up being stolen, for the very reason that they're popular. Can I put in a request for an inter-library loan for you?"

The lady stared at Ruth with a look on her face that implied her disgust. "You... you! You people NEVER have the book I'm looking for. Every time. Never mind!" She whirled on her heel and steamed out, clocking up the same speed at her exit as at her arrival, throwing back over her shoulder; "I'll just BUY the book. It'll be much faster than waiting for YOU to order if from another library."

Ruth let loose a long breath of air when the lady had disappeared down the stairs, her heels clicking loudly on the tiles as she headed for the front door.

Olivia had no clue. She really didn't. On a whim, Ruth grabbed a piece of scrap paper and scribbled: If she were a regular patron, I'd believe her frustration. However, I don't think I've even seen her in here before! She slipped it in the money drawer and returned to her work.

She continued the process of checking in the books, DVDs, audiobooks, and magazines that were waiting for her. At the check-out side of the desk, her colleague Serena was already checking out a regular. Elderly, with silvery white hair and a gentlemanly manner, he rarely chatted with the library clerks but always remembered their names.

"Thank you, Serena. Have a lovely day."

"If only they were ALL like that," Ruth murmured in Serena's direction as he left.

Serena grinned. "But life would be so much less dramatic, Ruth!"

Ding! The elevator arrived on the adult circulation floor and opened to admit a couple that Ruth had never seen together in the library, though the female looked slightly familiar. The male of the two was dressed entirely in black, cowboy boots included. A long trench coat completed his outfit. The female wore a Fruit-of-the-Loom white t-shirt, the type that comes in a multi-pack, ancient baggy jeans, circa at least a decade ago, and Birkenstock rip-offs. Internet users. Ruth watched them wander into the reference department, where the public computers were located. After discovering they needed a library card in order to surf the net, the pair headed in her direction.

Serena was occupied with putting away books, so Ruth took a deep breath. "Hello, how may I help you today?"

He flashed her a charming smile. His teeth were sharp and white, not dissimilar to a vampire's. "Hi. I've never had a library card before and I decided that it's about time!" he announced smoothly.

His companion had a pair of earbuds lodged in her ears. Jolting metallic sounds issued forthwith.

Ruth drew from the drawer the materials she needed to issue him with a library card. "Have you had a library card here before?"

"No, ma'am, I haven't. Maria has, but it was a long time ago, when she was a child."

"I need to see a form of I.D. as well as something with your name and current address on it."

"Well, I've just moved in the last two days, so I don't have anything with my name and address on it yet."

Ruth relented. He was so unusually well-spoken and polite, in spite of his dubious companion. "That's fine. Just bring one in as soon as you can! I'll put a note on your card to have one of us remind you."

He filled out his application form quickly, pausing once to ask the female a question.

"Huh?" she replied loudly. He repeated his question. She pulled out the earbud closest to him in order to hear his query for the third time. Music filled the space for a moment, until he'd received a sufficient reply and she'd plugged the device back into her ear, quieting but not muting the incessant noise.

Soon he had his card in his pocket and Ruth had entered his information into the computer. She wished them both a good day and they went on their way in the direction of the public computers.

She examined the card he'd filled out. The girl's name had clearly been given as his reference. Maria Steele. Ruth looked up her name in the patron database and was not surprised at the result. Eighty-nine dollars in library fines. Four unreturned library books. Two lost DVDs. All incidents dated less than ten months ago.

A long time ago indeed! Ruth scribbled again on the paper in the money drawer. We hear the same lies again and again. The amazing thing is, the people telling them think they're being original. Lies are never original. The truth certainly is!

She looked up to see Serena walking towards the circulation desk, away from the direction of the 700s shelves. A study table for the convenience of the patrons was located there. Serena was carrying a chair. Uh-oh. Has a toilet trip—challenged patron left us a present?

Serena's expression certainly indicated that they had. "I'm off to find the Lysol," she announced as she passed by.

Ruth could clearly see a dark mark on the cloth of the chair. She wrinkled her nose and wrote again in the paper. Cleaning up number two stains are all in a days' work at the library! I'm supposing you lawyers do that too? She allowed herself a tiny giggle but didn't have time to write more, for even as she heard the sound of Serena muttering to herself and scrubbing the chair in the staff room, a more demanding sound caught her ears. A horde approaching. Genghis Khan and his army?

Cynthia Walters and her three boys tumbled from the elevator in a cacophony of whines, thumps, and the calm voice of Cynthia, directing and encouraging. The boys hit the floor of the library running. One raced towards the world globe near the adult fiction shelves and began spinning it wildly. Another tripped and fell almost immediately, skinning his knee in a painful-looking carpet burn. The third, Dominic, turned around and headed back for the elevator, shutting himself in as his mother dealt with his wounded brother.

Ruth always wanted to help, but she did not know how. Cynthia's boys were triplets and Ruth, who admired Cynthia, could not conceive how on earth the woman stayed sane.

The elevator was dinging repeatedly, begging for help. Cynthia heard, and was matter-of-fact. "Dominic's intentionally shut himself in the elevator again. He did this on Saturday when we came in. It's his new thing. He'll ask us for help when he realizes he's stuck."

To the background of the dings, Cynthia, carrying the injured boy, grabbed two books from the shelf full of recent releases and helped the other child choose a DVD. The elevator was still singing when she returned to it with two of her boys in tow.

Ruth heard her say, "Oh, hello, Dominic. I'm afraid you missed choosing the DVD. Never mind, Michael and Robert chose a Thomas the Tank movie that I'm sure you'll love."

The elevator door closed to the sound of a sudden roar from Dominic. There was silence, and then, drifting up from the ground floor came roars and screams as the elevator opened and the family headed for the front door. Through it all Ruth could hear Cynthia's calm voice: "Next time, Dominic! Next time."

Maybe next time will be Saturday, on my day off, wrote Ruth, as she scribbled the story on her increasingly crumpled paper. She took a few deep breaths and spent five minutes putting away books that had accumulated.

At the sound of keys jingling at the front desk, she peered round the stacks to see a woman standing there. She carried a laptop bag.

"Miss?" The woman was already speaking as Ruth made her way back to the front desk.

"Yes? May I help you?"

"Well, I'm wantin' to see about having the internet put on my laptop. Someone told me you people did that down here?"

Ruth took a deep breath and let it out quietly before speaking. "You are welcome to connect to our wireless and use the internet while you're here."

"Will it still be on my laptop when I get home?"

"No. You have to have an internet provider and pay for your own monthly internet usage at home."

The woman stood for a moment, appearing confused. "You mean I can use it here, but when I git home it won't be there anymore?"

"Yes, that's right." Ruth did not know what else to say. She felt a murmur of hilarity rise up in her chest, but pushed it down.

"Well. I don't know what to do here. Somebody done told me you'ns could help me put internet on my new laptop."

"You can definitely use it while you're here, if you want to." Ruth settled the woman at a study table and showed her how to connect to the wireless and open an internet search engine.

All was quiet for a few minutes. Ruth put the remaining books away and settled herself in front of a stack of overdue book notices, waiting to be inserted in envelopes for mailing. She speedily wrote a few more paragraphs of notes about her day before she started folding the overdue notices.

"Miss?" The internet lady was there. "I'm trying to start up an email address. I gotta do it to git the free games I'm wantin'. Can you show me what to do?"

Free classes for novice internet users are not in our job description, but we do it anyway, Ruth scribbled in her notes, twenty minutes later.

She returned to folding her notices, feeling the same sadness she always felt when skimming over the titles of library materials that they'd probably never see again. Suddenly she became aware of someone standing in front of the circulation desk. How long they'd been there, she didn't know, as they'd said nothing and she'd been absorbed in her work. She looked up. A young man of around eighteen stood there. He grinned at her as she met his gaze.

"Hey," he greeted her.

Our Romeos often appear too, especially on romantically sunny days. They are all skulking admirers who somehow feel that having a library clerk as their other half would complete them. Easy to dissuade, thankfully. Just a little bit of simple —rejection— does it.

She raised her eyebrows at him. "Hello. Can I help you?"

He began a sort of strut alongside the desk. "I certainly hope so. I don't think I've seen you here before. How long have you been workin' here?"

This, coming on the date of Ruth's fifth year of work at the library, was too much. The bubble of mirth that she'd been pushing down throughout the morning threatened to burst and she nearly giggled. "A long time. I don't work Saturdays. You must be a Saturday patron."

"Saturday patron. That's me. But I'm so glad I decided to drop in on a Monday." He waited.

She sat, stony-faced, and repeated her question. "Can I help you?"

Serena breezed past, chair in hand. "Lunchtime for you, Ruth! I finally got the crap off this chair," she sang out, merrily.

Romeo stopped short in his strut and stared at Serena. "Hey," he said to her, in a low voice.

Ruth snatched her crumpled notes and retreated to the back room for lunch. She spent her lunch hour writing fast and furiously, laughing to herself as she wrote. After lunch, the entire afternoon passed in a whirl of activity. Right before closing time, there was a lull and Ruth found herself speed-reading a few pages of a new book. She remembered Olivia's words and laughed to herself. Reading novels all day indeed!

Monday patrons, morning-only roster:

Temperamental, at least 1.

Internet-challenged, 1.

Toilet-challenged, evidence of 1.

Truth-challenged, definitely more than 2.

Rivals to Genghis Khan, 3.

Amorous,.

"Normal," 15

Saturday morning arrived, and with it Ruth's usual coffee date with Olivia at Constellations Coffee House. They ordered their customary pot of French press coffee to share and seated themselves comfortably at one of the sofas. Ruth presented Olivia with a slightly crumpled paper. "Here you are, Liv. My Monday notes upon reaching the anniversary of five years of work at the library."

She sat back and drank deep gulps of the strong coffee as Olivia read quietly.

"Whew, Ruth!" Olivia had clearly finished. She shook her head. "Maybe you don't get paid enough for what you do," she admitted, looking serious. "I'd definitely be wanting a raise after all that. I would have never thought —at the library!"

"It's just… working with the public, Olivia. Surely you know all about it. All in a day's work!"

## THE CATALPA TREE SQUIRREL
### A.J. Gardner

I watched this squirrel from my window. He'd wanted to leap from the catalpa tree to the tree across the driveway.

He ran down the limb several times, then looked toward the ground below. He went back up the limb and thought it over awhile, shaking his tail. Finally, he went out on another limb that was closer to the tree across the drive. He looked down once more than made his big leap and landed safely on the other side.

It taught me that I'd better look before I leap, since I'd made some bad leaps in the past.

The ground is hard when you land at that distance, and you finally learn, but by that time, it's generally too late.

## DO YOU BELIEVE?
### Pauline Mangin

Growing up as a young girl life was not easy for my family. We lived on the poor south-side of Orion on the corner of Michigan and Goodlet Streets. My family consisted of three older sisters, one younger brother, my aunt, and my mother. My middle sister and I hung around most of the time. We were the tomboys of the family. We got into trouble a lot and were accused even when we weren't guilty.

One bright and early morning around seven a.m., my sister and I met her best friend from school. We were just hanging around being kids when we discovered a vacant house. It was a very small house that should have been condemned. My sister and her friend peered through small dark windows on the front of the house but couldn't see inside. They tried wiping off the windows but still they couldn't see through the darkness.

We went to a door on the back of the house and slowly turned the doorknob and walked into what must have been the kitchen. I was alarmed to discover that someone had painted all the windows in the house black. As I walked round the corner into the living room, I noticed something strange out of the corner of my eye. I wasn't sure if I was seeing things or not, so I moved closer to get a better view.

I was horrified by the sight. There was a very frail looking old lady in her eighties or nineties sitting in a rocking chair rocking back and forth, back and forth. She had dirty gray hair, deep sunken eyes, and very thin skin. I saw two knitting needles sticking out of her head.

She opened to speak and I could see the two needles crisscross inside her mouth.

I screamed and ran from the house. To my surprise my sister and her friend had followed me out. A crowd of people had gathered in the street and yelled at us as we ran, "What are you kids doing in there? You kids need to stay away from the house! You kids should go home and stay away!" We ran but we didn't go home. I wasn't sure about all the yelling or exactly what I thought I'd seen. Perhaps I was dreaming. I wasn't sure why my sister and her friend had followed me from the house; they hadn't seen what I had. Perhaps the house just spooked them.

I never told my sisters or my mother what I had seen that day. Several weeks later we returned. To our surprise the house had been torn down, and all that remained was a vacant lot.

Some people believe in supernatural creatures such as ghosts, zombies, and vampires, but I know what I saw. Memories of that day will forever be etched in my mind and that is where they will stay.

## THE CHRISTMAS MEDAL
©2008, C. Byron Buckley

The embers glowed softly, and in their dim light,
Shadows leaped and danced in a playful sight.
My wife was asleep, her head on my chest,
My daughter beside me, angelic in rest

Outside the snow fell, a blanket of white
And covered all of nature in a winter delight.
The sparkling lights in the tree, I believe,
Completed the magic that was Christmas Eve

The sound wasn't loud, and it wasn't too near,
But I opened my eyes when it tickled my ear.
Perhaps just a cough, I didn't quite know,
Then the crunch of footsteps outside in the snow.

My soul gave a tremble, I struggled to hear,
And I crept to the door just to see who was near.
Standing out in the cold and the dark of the night,
A lone figure stood, his face weary and tight.

A soldier, I puzzled, some twenty years old,
Perhaps a Marine, huddled here in the cold.

Alone in the dark, he saluted and smiled,
"I'm watching over you, your wife and child."

I've not seen my own son in more than a while,
But my wife sends pictures and he has her smile.
Then he bent and he carefully pulled from his bag,
The red, white, and blue... a folded American flag.

It's hard but I could carry the weight of killing another,
And I could lay down my life for my sister and brother
Who stand bravely at the front against one and all,
To ensure for all time that this flag will not fall.

I turned and looked at the photograph of my son
In his uniform with the medal that he had won
And when I turned to address my protector
He had disappeared like a ghostly specter
Then my daughter's curls bounced down every stair
And she announced without hesitation or care:
"Daddy, I heard you talking to Rudolph and those other reindeer."
"Yes, my dear, they certainly brought you lots of Christmas cheer."
"Daddy, Daddy, what's this medal doing under our tree?"

## THE UNDECORATED CHRISTMAS TREE
©2014 C. Byron Buckley

Her teenage eyes would have seen where
Each ornament would have been placed with care
The tree, like life itself, awaited
But her youthful touch is gone and abated
Although in the corner sits a dark tree,
She gave her eyes so another could suddenly see
Out of this dark tragedy comes another's luminosity
So let's cherish her and decorate her tree
Her youthful soul can light the way
For others to know Heaven's endless day.

   – This poem was requested by a former student, Bonnie Dailey Page, and was read at her granddaughter's funeral – a teenager who was killed in a tragic car accident on her way home from work. This young girl had planned to decorate the family's Christmas tree when she returned home after work that night. She donated her eyes so a blind person could see for the first time. This was one of the most difficult poems that I had to quickly write or ever write.

# BAMBIES
A.J. Gardner
Written 12-13-14

There are lots of Bambies at the Ole Farm Place.
Sometimes you see a dozen or more,
and at other times, you see sixteen just to
even the score.

When they finally see you or me, they let out a
snort or two, and into the woods thy flee.

If you plant a garden, don't think they'll stay away.
Right down the okra row, that's where they love to play.
They come out of the woods, leap the creek and
Under the pines they glide.

And when they're eating that okra and spitting all over,
You can tell they love that stuff even better than clover.

Then, when under the pines they glide,
I often wonder which ones will come back,
As the neighbors value their hides.

## BROKEN PROMISES
### Brooke Kavanaugh

He said he'd be back in an hour,
With a rose for me to hold
While we danced and he spun me in circles,
Like he would never let me go
As a smile tugged at my lips
With laughter in the air
And a sparkle in my eye,
Like fireworks on the Fourth of July.
He swore that I would
Love his gift.
That nothing would ever compare
But that I would have to wait,
Because in order for me to receive it,
He had to retrieve it.
And I still remember,
I still remember the look
On his face as he left:
The teasing smile,
The little wave of his hand,
The undeniable twinkle in his emerald eyes,
Like he had a secret no one else knew.

He opened his car door,
Slid inside,
And drove off,
Leaving me there,
Counting the minutes
As they passed by,
Too excited to let anything
Ruin this moment.
But I stood there,
Rubbing my arms and bouncing on my toes,
Too anxious to stand still
Even though I had been
Waiting and
Waiting and
Waiting.
Because that's what love is
I kept telling myself,
It's patient
And kind
And forgiving.
…or so I thought.
And as time slipped away,
I held on to the hope that
He would come back.
He would come back
With his teasing smile
And his promise of a gift
And his promise of a dance
And his promise of spinning me in circles
And his promise of making me laugh
And his promise of never letting me go.
But he never did.
He never came back.
And I have never been angrier.

Why?
Why did you leave me?
What did I ever do to deserve this?
A hopeless, broken heart
So devoid of any emotion except anger
That I am unable
To form any type
Of affection for others
As I had done with you.
I had allowed the walls
That had guarded
And protected
My heart
To fall.
Because you had torn them down
Piece by piece.
When you left, you had been my foundation.
When you left, I crumbled to the ground.
 I had been so dependent,
With you by my side
Because I had someone to trust
Because I had someone to lean on
Because I had someone to support me
Because I had someone to catch me when I fell,
That when you left,
I no longer knew how to stand on my own.
But I still remember,
I still remember
When your mom approached me
With tears streaming down her face
As I stood in front of your casket.
She whispered to me,
That due to the force of the impact
Between the two cars, that when you flew

Through the windshield of your car,
That this fell out of your pocket.
And in my empty hand,
She placed a small box.
But I didn't open it there.
I was too angry
Too frustrated
Too confused
Too blinded by the love that I once had!
But when I finally opened it,
I had never been more surprised.
Because inside the box,
Was a shiny golden ring.
That was your gift, wasn't it?
You were going to propose to me.
And even now,
When I know that you're dead,
I still wear your ring.
I still hang on to your broken promises.
I haven't let go.
Because one day,
One day,
You're going to find
Your way back home.

## SILENT NIGHT
### Mary B. Goss

The house was silent. Sue Ann heaved a sigh of relief as her six-year old tornado-of-a-grandson slept. Blessed peace enveloped her on the couch and she sat for a moment and rested her sixty year-old bones that screamed for relief. Playing soccer wasn't so bad on a Saturday afternoon, but football, too, just about finished her off.

A cup of hot tea and cookies to dunk revived her. Having her grandson was a blessing and her responsibility required pacing herself and her soul. Lord, she was tired. Samuel didn't lack for anything, though, while he waited for his parents to grow up. Letter in hand, she sipped her tea and began her nightly prayers for the parents. Her son, the dad, wrote weekly from jail, a father who preferred addictions to accepting responsibility for the boy. The mom now wrote long letters about finding herself and finding a job and finding a man and by the way here's a birthday card and a promise of a dollar for her son. Sue Ann let the letters fall unopened from her hand. Tomorrow she would sleep in. No, tomorrow she would take Samuel to church and hope that God's goodness and grace would protect them all. Tomorrow she would slit the legal envelope and wade through the fine print. Tonight she had hope for Samuel's birthday and clothes to pull from the dryer.

The music rocked the windows, the laughter shook the lights as six boys played holiday games and the half dozen girls giggled. She had forgotten how much children giggled. And Samuel was the loudest. The church group in Orion sponsored a combined holiday birthday part and it was a success. Two birthday cakes graced the table, one for Samuel and one for baby Jesus. How had she ever gotten by without the generosity of strangers? Yes, she had pride but she surrendered it, so Samuel could have the basic safety, security and stability needed. And he had love.  Share the love and obey rules were her mantra and Samuel wanted to share his day with baby Jesus and everyone. Samuel was outgrowing her. It was the last party where he would sit and wear funny hats and eat cake and giggle. Next year, he would want his friends or a pizza party and events that didn't allow old faces to sit at the table. But she banished that storm of worry and vowed to enjoy today.

The doorbell rang. Samuel turned away because he knew there was no one to come for him.

Sue Ann swung open the door.

Surprise replaced her pleasure and her anger boiled.

Two policemen stood on the steps along with Samuel's mother and another couple.

"Sorry, ma'am but they have a court order."

"You didn't respond to my last letter, "the woman hissed.

"Who is it, grandma?" Samuel's voice echoed down the hall.

Pain warred with pity. Sue Ann said a quick prayer and did the only Christian thing she knew to do.

She invited them all inside.

An hour later, the policemen left with cake and autographs and going along with the ruse that they were specials guests since Samuel wanted to be a policemen. Samuel's grandparents were an added surprise, but it was Mom who won the spot of honor.

Three hours later, Sue Ann lit her candle against the evening dark and began her evening prayers. In the darkness, the Christmas lights flickered. Samuel departed with his mother, supervised by the grandparents in a carload of gifts leaving behind a disaster of birthday debris.

Tomorrow she would sleep in before opening her present. Fool that she was, she had no legal papers to protect her rights and no paper could protect her heart. She threw the legal summons into the fire and knew she would not fight the mother for custody. As the papers turned to ashes, Sue Ann fingered her present, and unrolled the paper drawing of baby Jesus by Samuel.

She stood and walked to the kitchen. She'd place it on the refrigerator once her traitorous fingers let go of the fingerpainted duo of Samuel holding baby Jesus while an old angel labeled grandma looked on.

Sue Ann paused and savored the gift. After all, she'd shared the love and obeyed the rules. She gave the finest Christmas gift of all to Samuel. She'd kept the faith.

She let him go.

# THANK YOU
## Vince Sellers

I was crying as I stared into the campfire, not a hard cry, just a weeping that didn't seem to want to stop. My hard crying had come earlier when I realized my father was dead. A death brought on by cancer. Lung cancer. Drowning a slow death is what it was. I was driven to go home to my father's farm, a few miles southeast of Orion. I could see the lights of the town off in the distance when I stepped away from the fire. My father and I had gathered here many times when we went coon hunting, but I hadn't coon hunted in years. I was too busy in the world off the farm. Dad and I would talk of his dog, Old Ted, when Dad was young. Ted was considered by many to be the best coon dog in the county. Old Ted had been Dad's dog since Dad was a teenager. I sold my own dogs when I had gone off to college, years ago now....

I was staring into the campfire remembering my father's struggles as he lay dying. The doctors had been checking on his legs after his first round of chemo and radiation. For some reason his legs were bothering him. The doctor's decided to check his lungs as part of the process. It was not good. The doctor in charge had gathered Dad's children, all adults now, and told us the bad news in the hallway outside of Dad's haring. When I returned to Dad's room, Dad insisted I tell him what the doctor had said.

"You aren't going to make it, Dad", was my grim reply. "The cancer has come back in your lungs and there is nothing the doctors can do."

Later, I was in the room when my older brother, who is very religious, was visiting. He was reminding Dad of the reason for Christ's death on the cross. Christ's death was to help us be with God in heaven, to open the gates so to speak. He emphasized to Dad, "Just remember, Dad, when you get to the other side, you must look for Jesus. You know that is why He came here on earth to guide us to Him when we die."

So the vigil began; each of us taking turns being with Dad. I noted that despite Dad's pain, he was always polite to his caregivers. He would look them in the eye and get their attention and say firmly "thank you" for any consideration they would provide him. He insisted on a clock being in the room. Once, when his oxygen was low and the caretakers had not noticed, he struggled and tossed and turned. I was with my sister in the room at the time. I heard Dad mumbling under his breath. I leaned in closely and thought I heard the prayers of the rosary. "Do you want us to say a rosary," I asked. Dad shook his head yes. And so the rosary became part of Dad's ritual toward death.

My Dad got better when the oxygen problem was fixed, but only for a while. I noticed that Dad did arm exercises to improve his strength, even though there was no hope that he would ever get out of his sick bed. The end came after six weeks of struggle. Just after Dad took his last breath I said, "Remember to look for Jesus on the other side."

The funeral would wait a few days while we gathered relatives from all over the country. After I made the last calls to family, I had the overwhelming urge to return to the home place. I wanted to be alone with my thoughts and my grief.

I sat at the camp-fire thinking and praying and sometimes just listening to the night. I really hadn't come out to do this, but it just seemed like the right thing for me to do once I got there that night.

As I sat looking and thinking and trying not to feel anything, I was startled to hear a dog off in the distance. It was a coon dog. Someone was hunting in the area. The sound grew nearer. I did not hear the teenager come up to the fire. He was there on the edge of the light. The kid asked to come closer. I hesitated; the kid had a gun. A shotgun. The breach was open. After a few moments, I told the kid to come and sit down.

The kid said, "Thanks, I was getting a little cold. "That's my dog running," he added.

"What's his name," I asked.

"Ted" was the reply.

I jumped a little when the kid said Ted, and I looked a little closer at him in the glow of the firelight. The kid stood by the fire and would not sit down, but kept looking intently at me. I grew uneasy with the stare. "You okay?" I inquired of the boy.

"Yes, I am fine, now." The kid laughed. It was a joyful laugh. "I am more OK than you can know," the kid added.

"I am sorry I don't have anything to offer you," I said, "I had not planned to come here tonight; did it on the spur of the moment."

The kid nodded. Suddenly his dog came into the firelight. He came right up to me and licked my boot and then my face. The teenager laughed and called out, "Ted, settle down with that and come heel. Heel I said." The dog came over and sat behind the kid.

"Well, I am warmed up enough," the kid said. "I better get on with it. Up." he yelled at the dog, and off the dog jumped running away into the darkness. The kid watched him go. I felt disconcerted not having anything to offer the kid, and said so to him. The kid turned around in the glow of the firelight and looked me square in the eyes and said, "You have done enough, THANK YOU" the kid added with emphasis, then turned and walked away into the darkness.

I watched him go, then realized I didn't know the kid's name. I walked out into the darkness and yelled for him, but the kid did not reply. The dog had been calling, but suddenly his howling and yelping bark ceased. All was quiet again. I returned to the fire and paced back and forth, not sure of what had just happened. It was all too strange. I finally kicked dirt upon the fire and put it out, returned to my car, and went home to Orion. I told my wife about the kid and the dog on the home place. My wife listened but did not offer any explanation.

The next night we gathered at my sister's home. We had all the old photos scattered on the kitchen table trying to pick the best ones for the funeral home display the following night. We laughed and we cried as they looked through all the old photos. Suddenly I saw a photo that turned me white as a sheet.

"Who is this in the photo," I asked my oldest sister. It's Dad as a teenager with his favorite coon dog, Old Ted," my sister replied.

I turned to my wife and told her, "This is the boy at the fire, and this is the dog he had with him." There was no doubt in my mind. Dad had made one last visit to thank me and tell me he had indeed found what he was looking for on the other side.

I smiled and said "We'll put this photo of Dad and Ted with the collage at the funeral home." And, so we did.

## POTATO BUGS
### Roy L. Wachter

I was eight years old and in second grade. School was out for the summer. I lived with my parents and little sister in a house that was on top of a hill about one mile outside Orion, Indiana. To get to our house we needed to wind up and up for about a mile. The house was very simple with an outdoor toilet and a hand pump to raise water from a cistern that collected rain water from our roof.

Dad had purchased the little house and five acres. He immediately purchased a mule, named old Charley, built chicken coops in the old barn and started to plow what little land that was almost level. One thing he did with the plowed land was to plant a potato garden. By June the potato plants had grown to about one-foot tall; however, beetles that Dad called the "potato bugs," began consuming the lush leaves on most plants.

My Dad worked for the railroad and spent many hours away from his little farm. That left the task of removing the bugs from the potatoes to my mother. Reluctantly my mother picked each little bug and placed them in a paper bag. The potato bugs immediately climbed the sides of the bag to escape to eat another day. Milk in that day always came in glass bottles. She replaced the paper bag with one of those bottles. The inside of the glass bottle was too slippery for the tiny bug feet to grip; thus they remained in a pile at the bottom of milk bottle.

I helped pick the potato bugs until my bottle was almost full. "What do I do now? I asked.

"Burn them in the burn-barrow."

"Where are the matches?" I asked.

"On second thought, I don't want you playing with matches. Pour some gasoline on them."

"Where is the gasoline?"

"I don't think your dad has any in the shed. Besides I don't want you messing with gasoline either. You'll have to use rubbing alcohol instead."

I finally located the alcohol on a shelf in the closet under the basement steps. Back upstairs in the kitchen I carefully poured the alcohol into the bottle and watched the bugs swim about. Wanting to get a better view of the bugs I poured about 30 out onto the planks of the kitchen table.

I was amazed as I saw several bugs attempt to crawl across the table. They wobbled from side to side; obviously they were drunk. I had to laugh. Then eight of the bugs collected in the center of a ring formed by the other bugs. The eight seemed to be square dancing. After a bit they regrouped and danced the Virginia Reel. The potato bugs that formed the surrounding ring seemed to sway to some imaginary music. I had to abandon the entertainment and go to my mother when she called from the garden.

When I returned to the kitchen table, all activity had ceased. All the potato bugs lay in one pile. The bugs were scattered into some type of pattern. I starred at the scattered bugs until I could make out the letter "T." Then, I noticed the letter "Y." My mouth fell open when I realized the potato bugs had spelled out the words, "Thank You."

I never told my mother. I never told anyone until now. You're the first to hear the story. I think you can understand.

## RAINY DAYS
### Larry Mattes

I love the rain that falls in our lives
It reminds me of the times that are special
The times that we take just for ourselves
The times for just you and me and the rain

The gentle rains are the times for our walks
To feel the wetness against our skin, walking together
To laugh and splash like children in the puddles
To kiss and embrace in the sweetness of the rain

The thunderstorms are the times for cozy fires
Resting in my arms and feeling the warmth of desire
Feeling the security of being lost in my love
Listening to the pounding of the rain and our hearts

The lightning flashes across the dark skies
It lights up the room and highlights your smile
You bring a glow to both my heart and my life
Those brief interludes of light illuminate your love

As the thunder outside rumbles ever so near
It is like the love inside me that yearns for release

Building and building and growing stronger each day
Till like the crash of the thunder, my passion explodes

I love the rain that falls in our lives
I love the feelings that that each storm provides
You and I live for each storm that comes by
Oh my dear the rain says I love you all over again

## THE RAINMAKER AND THE PREACHER
Connie Carroll

I will be 115 years old this year, quite unlikely you are probably thinking. Yes, that would be true if my skeleton was made of calcium, and my skin was made of billions of dermis cells. If my feet had ten phalanges and my crowning glory made me a redhead, brunette, or blonde. However you see that is not the case. Let me describe myself a little better. My skeleton is made of red oak, one of the hardest woods to be found, and my skin is made up of hand-made fired clay bricks. My feet have no phalanges, but have heart of pine planks, shined to gloss of the sweat on a roan horse's back. But perhaps my best feature, my crowning glory, is the magnificent copper gilt that sets at my very top, and can be seen from miles around. I suppose by now you have guessed that indeed, I am not human, although I too was born through labor pain. If you have the time and are so inclined to listen, I would like to share with you a little of how I came to be.

Although the date of my birth is technically Dec 24, 1900, I was conceived in a farmer's pasture on a June evening so humid that the mosquitoes didn't even have the motivation to bite. Sweet tea was being passed around but it could not quench the heat still lingering from the day, nor the fervor of the participants. A large tent had been constructed in the early afternoon and at least 100 souls were present for the event. It was the first night of the Revival of the Followers of Jesus of Orion, Indiana. This was to be an especially important revival due to some recent unpleasantness in the town. It had been a tough summer for the growing community, as there had not been any real measurable rain since the middle of May. Now for an area where crop farming made up a large part of the economy this was not a good situation. The unpleasantness began shortly after the town council voted to hire a "rainmaker." They hired one, Earnest I. Willowby, Rainmaker Extraordinaire, to help with the lack of precipitation. Unfortunately, it seems no one on the council had checked Mr. Ernest I. Willowby's credentials.

The endeavor seemed to start off well enough. Mr. Willowby made a grand speech on the town square, proclaiming that by the end of the week, the good people of Orion would not be able to leave their homes without a bumbershoot. Oh, how excited everyone was with anticipation of full ponds, cisterns, and running streams. Talk of how the crops and gardens would all be saved could be heard on every front porch in town, and along the dusty roads beyond the ends of the sidewalks. Monday, Mr. Ernest I. Willowby began setting up his rainmaking equipment on the edge of town. This being that certain fumes might be emitted to insure the deluge that the council had requested, and Mr. Willowby did not want to subject the fine folks of Orion with any olfactory discomfort. Most of that first day was taken up with the setting of a vast cooper structure that resembled a wash tube with a chimney. When questioned about this Ernest I. just stated that it was needed to heat the "air particles." It appeared on Tuesday that several coils of tubing were added to the now growing apparatus. The curious, anxious folks of Orion continued to watch in awe as their hopes for rain grew with the size of rain making machine. Wednesday brought a request from the rainmaker for several cords of wood to be brought to the site. He explained that he would need to keep a steady fire to make sure the "air particles kept moving. So in the heat of the June days, several farmers cut and hauled wood for the process. It was on Thursday that the strangest request yet was made by Ernest I. It seems he needed bushels of dry corn to finish up the last step of the rainmaking. So again the town pulled together and rounded up enough dry corn left from the last Fall's harvest. At last on Friday, the now impatient citizens were pleased when the fire was lit, the corn was put in the kettle and water added, so the "air particles" could begin to diffuse, dance and produce rain! It seemed like a holiday, with children teasing, people slapping each other on the back and joking, "now don't look up too long at the rain, or you might drown." Yes, spirits were high.

All day the sky was watched; surely the air particles would come together and a black rain cloud would appear. Eyestrain began to appear but no clouds. The day wore on just as dusty hot and humid as the ones before, and still no rain. The only thing falling in Orion was folks' hopes. The night went on and even as the fumes from the rainmaking machine grew stronger, the stars twinkled on. It was close to noon on Saturday when the first inkling of the coming unpleasantness appeared. At about that time old Ben B. sure hit town for his weekly grocery stop. The crowd around the rainmaking machine had grown to be quite large. Just a little speculation had also grown, as to how wise the town council had been in engaging Mr. Ernest I. Willowby, Rainmaker Extraordinaire. Well, old Ben asked a few people about the goings on, and the waiting crowd explained about the kettle, tubes, wood, and corn. Ben listened then slowly made his way to the front of the gathering. He looked around, sniffed the air, and with a perplexed expression declared, "Why in tarnation is the town of Orion paying this man to make moonshine at the edge of town!"

"No!" the cry went up! "He is going to make it rain."

"Well, that's funny," said old Ben B. Sure, cause he looks a lot like the fella that got thrown in jail last week over in Daviess county for running 'shine." By this time the good duped citizens of Orion, had arranged a ride out of town for Mr. Ernest I Willowby. It was a specially designed rail ride which would go in only one direction.

Now back to my conception. A week or so after the departure of the "rainmaker," a traveling revival preacher came to Orion. The sky was still blue as cornflowers in a spring pasture, not a splatter of rain had been felt. After the preacher had heard about the rainmaker, he stated, "What this town needs is a revival and I will be happy to conduct that for you." It is not hard to imagine that after their hopes had been dashed so cruelly, the faithful of Orion weren't too sure about the preacher. He had not promised them rain, just a revival. So a tent was set up, chairs arranged, songs sung, the plate passed and the preacher commenced to preaching. Now folks in this area were used to and prepared for a little fire and brimstone, but this preacher was a different. The crickets and tree frogs even seemed to silence their evening sounds as the preacher confidently gave his message. He spoke of a message from the Bible that the folks in a farming community could relate to. It told of how with faith as small as a mustard seed, prayer can be answered. He then asked those gathered, if they had that faith, and with a couple of spontaneous "Amens," some powerful praying began. Well, then nothing happened and all went home. But undoubtedly more prayer was said as bedtime came. Those who stayed up late that evening said the first thing they noticed was a change in the air. The humidity seemed to fall and a freshening breeze kicked up. Then the smell, the one that can only be one thing: rain coming across a pasture. It started slow and the collected breath of Orion was held, to see if enough would come to save the crops. It rained through the night and into the middle of the next day.

Tradition says that those who prayed in that tent in the farmer's pasture that June evening promised that they would build a fine church in Orion in thanksgiving for blessings received. The somewhat unique component of this promise was that the faithful agreed that the church would be built regardless whether the much needed rain came or not. So that is how I was conceived. I was born through the labor of the people of Orion, who brought the red oak for my framing, clay brick for my skin the heart of pine for my floors and the copper for my steeple. I may be 115 years old, but the faithful still worship in my loving embrace and give thanks for all their blessings.

## DUFF, MY HOME TOWN
### Gordon Hochmeister

Few people have been born into a community where "mas, pas, uncles, and aunts" were actually not kinfolk at all. I learned in a few short years that the people who I called by these names reserved the right to inflict corporal punishment upon me when I was caught in their presence committing an infraction that was not acceptable. Then they would file a report with my parents and the punishment moved up a step or two.

I was born in Duff, Indiana (Dubois County), about twenty-five miles southeast of Orion. The date was June 30, 1942, just over six months after the attack on Pearl Harbor. I was born at home, two doors south of Wayne Hall's (grocery) Store and two doors north of the Southern Railway tracks. My earliest memories were of the troop trains that traveled the railway after World War II was declared. I was the youngest of the four children of Lewis and Edna Hochmeister, and my father, like many other able-bodied males, was drafted into the United States Navy at almost thirty years of age. After training at the Great Lakes Naval Station, he became a gunner on the "Mad" Anthony Wayne, a supply ship that was infamous for being attacked virtually every time it hit the water. He served three years in the European Theater before returning to his family in Duff in 1945.

Our little four-room frame house was located on an alley that dissected the over-sized city block that made up Duff, home to approximately fifty residents. Everyone knew everyone. If you saw Ben Gearner, he was usually under the influence of "white lightning." The "gentleman farmer," cigar-smoking Dick Lemond, was never without his white shirt, khaki slacks, and the appropriate fedora for the season. Ma and Pa Peach could be heard arguing from anywhere on the block. Kelso Hall operated the only competition for his father, Wayne Hall, by having a store on the southeast corner of the block.

Across the road from Wayne Hall's Store was the baseball field, where some pretty good Duff Indians baseball games were played, even playing against Gil Hodges, who was on a team from Petersburg during his off-seasons from the Brooklyn Dodgers. I watched Dad play many games with Jess Hall pitching and the other Duff athletes on the field.

On the north side of the Southern Railway tracks was the railway depot. Upon occasion, the depot served as an overnight inn to a hobo traveling through, waiting for a ride on the Southern Railway. Inside the door of the depot was a long bamboo stick with a red flag attached. Its purpose? To flag the freight train to a stop and board the passenger car for a five-cent trip to Huntingburg. To walk those tracks, even today, generates a flood of memories.

After the War, my Dad, along with the other veterans, returned home and picked up where he left off, working at Plant # 1 of the Huntingburg Furniture Company. I remember hearing him discuss his fellow-gunner and best friend, Hensley, but never did I hear him mention the War or anything connected to it. He joined the Veterans of Foreign Wars and the American Legion. I always felt that he needed to be with those who had "been there."

Dubois County was well known, at the time, for producing "white lightning," supplying the "speakeasies" of larger cities like Chicago. I can still remember my Dad standing out in the garden, smelling the air coming from the southeast and saying, "smells like ol' Vic is cookin' tonight." There were several known moonshiners within three to four miles of Duff. Though I can't mention names, after I moved to Orion, a guy I'll just call "Spike" said that he spent a night watching the production of some moonshine being manufactured by a customer who he supplied with seed corn.

Shortly after Dad's return from the war, we moved to a place that was known as the Rauscher Farm, located about a mile northeast of Duff via gravel road. It was a four-room frame house with an unfinished upper floor. There was also a basement, which the house in Duff did not have. But, once again, we were without some things: Central heat, running water and an indoor bathroom. Dad enjoyed the large garden space and spent his springs and summers there. The fresh vegetables helped feed a growing family, and Mom canned everything that we didn't eat from the garden. During the next few years, the family grew from six members to eight with the addition of my two brothers.

Soon after moving to the Rauscher Farm, I started school at Duff Elementary. The schoolhouse was located on a hill, approximately one-fourth mile north of Wayne Hall's Store. It was without "modern facilities." Since we were not on a school bus route, my two older sisters and I would either walk across the field to school or walk south to the corner and meet Paulie Davis taking his children to school in an enclosed horse-drawn milk wagon. It made those winter trips a lot warmer.

The school entry was a room where there were hooks to hang up coats, plus wash pans and a water bucket for maintaining cleanliness. This is also where the brown paper bags containing students' lunches were kept until lunch time. There was a large coal stove in the main room and desks that served grades 1 -8. That's right, in one room! That truly was a great advantage for learning, due to the younger students being able to eavesdrop on the classes of the older students. Huldah L. Cooper was an amazing teacher who taught us much more than learning from a book. I can still name the Presidents and the years they served up through Eisenhower. The Duff School was closed in 1954 and I started Junior High in Huntingburg. It was a shock to us "Duff Kids" to be in a big school like Huntingburg, but many of us became involved in athletics, music and other activities that the school provided. However, Duff was always home to the four of us in my grade.

Growing up on the Rauscher Farm was fun! I begged Mister Rauscher to let me work in the hay fields and he finally relented when I turned eleven. It was a summer job I held until I was in high school. The evenings were spent with a walk to Duff and a visit with friends at Wayne Hall's Store. Marvin Stapleton would be there, along with his two pet crows, Jim and Pete. Marvin could call for them by name, and here they'd come, seemingly out of nowhere, and land on his shoulder! His Irish Setter, Happy, wouldn't be far away. The time spent on that front porch and inside the store, listening to the men talk was always a treat for the young boys, though we were not permitted to participate unless asked. The memories prompted me to write a poem, fitly titled "Wayne Hall's Store."

The ev'ning air was lettuce crisp
My ragged shirt not warm enough,
I walked along and kicked at rocks
On the lonely road that led to Duff.

Once there and with the local boys
All finished with our ev'ning chore,
To entertain we'd gather on
The porch in front of Wayne Hall's Store.

We'd tease and laugh and tell tall tales,
Then walk across the oil-drenched floor
To take our place on church-type pews
'Round the pot-bellied stove at Wayne Hall's Store.

The fire a'cracklin' – a spread of warmth,
With list'ning ears we'd hope for more,
To learn things made for memories
'Round that pot-bellied stove at Wayne Hall's Store.


Money was sparse for our family, and my father and I started trapping animals for their fur. When the furs were sold near the end of November, our earnings became our "Christmas money." We also dug ginseng and yellow root and dried and sold it. I will never forget the closeness of our family and the work ethic developed by each of us.

When I was thirteen years old, my brother and I both received new bicycles for Christmas. I will never forget that surprise! That was the end of our WALKS to Duff!

I graduated from Huntingburg High School in May of 1960 and enlisted in the United States Army on June 29th, at the age of seventeen. After a three-year stint in the Army, I spent a career in law enforcement, raised a family, and finally settled into retirement. But I never completely left Duff....

In the mid-1990s I was contacted by the Duff Church of Christ, inviting me to speak at an evening service. As I spoke from the pulpit, I observed Ma Peach, well into her nineties, obviously uneasy in her seat, looking away from me, and acting angry. After the service, I went directly to her and asked what was wrong, thinking I said something offensive to her. Her reply, "I can't believe you were up there!" When I asked why, she said, "You were the meanest kid I ever knew." Hmmmm. She actually remembered that Halloween night and that burning brown paper bag on her front porch!"

There is one thing for sure: Duff will always be "Home" to me!

Compiled By: Roy L. Wachter

## FIFTH SUNDAY SURPRISE
### Wini Fagen Frances

Growing up in middle America, in what my parents called the buckle of the Bible belt, helped mold me into the person I am today. I called Orion, a small rural town buried in the hills, my home. It wasn't really a town because if you blinked you'd miss it. Maybe village or spot-in-the-road would be more fitting.

Typical of most small towns, everybody knew everyone else on a first name basis. They knew who was related to whom, and nosed into everyone's business. The latest nose report (the guys called it news) flowed from the old codgers sitting in the rockers on the front porch of the general store. If Sam drove home drunk from the city and stumbled into his home at 2:00 AM, they knew it by 7:00 AM when they gathered on the porch. If someone wanted to know if Madge's dog had her puppies yet, whether someone missed mid-week Bible study, or even when my dad spanked me, all they had to do was check in at the general store. The old guys discussed all this and more. They even argued about the best way for the President and Congress to solve the latest world problems.

My father Walter owned and operated the feed mill at the edge of town. He sealed business agreements with a handshake and always kept his word. He and mom instilled in me the Christian Biblical principles of respect, responsibility, honesty, morality, and the importance of keeping my word. I remember him telling me, "Remember whose you are. It takes years to build good character, a good reputation, and a good name. You have a good name, but you can lose it overnight. Think before you act."

We never missed a church service. My parents dragged me there even when I didn't want to go. When the church doors opened, we sat on the second pew from the front on the left-hand side. No padded pews and no air conditioning then. Dad taught Sunday school and challenged my class to memorize Scripture. Mom baked cookies and cooked for the monthly youth rallies. She headed up our summer vacation Bible school. Because the church played such a prominent role in my life, I wonder if that's why I married a minister. At the age of eighteen and one week after graduating from high school, I married my husband Mike, the only man and preacher I ever dated. We moved away from Orion, but visited several times a year. The church folks always wanted Mike to preach and me to lead the singing when we returned home to visit.

I loved 5th Sunday services growing up. They filled the whole day. Preaching in the morning and singing at the night service. We ate lots of yummy homemade chicken and noodles and fresh baked pies. Ham, fried chicken, sandwiches, and fresh-baked homemade yeast rolls graced the first table. Either juicy sliced red and yellow tomatoes straight from the garden, cabbage slaw, and wilted lettuce salad covered the second table, or home canned green beans, frozen buttered sweet corn cut off the cob, and pickled beets, depending on the time of year the 5th Sunday fell.

I'll never forget the last 5th Sunday service in which we participated. Mike preached a rousing sermon. The kids even talked about his illustrations. But it proved difficult for me to concentrate on the message. The overwhelming, delicious smelling aromas wafting up the basement stairs from the food carried in for the dinner distracted me. Visiting with friends and relatives and reacquainting myself with great nieces and nephews filled the afternoon. We enjoyed tasty leftovers for supper before the evening songfest.

The last 5th Sunday sing was unique and memorable. Dad's been gone over twenty years. But my wheelchair bound, arthritic Mom, who can't play the piano any more, attended the festivities. Since I was leading the singing, I decided to do something different. I told the congregation we were going to play a word association game. I would say the first word. Then the first person in the audience to think of a hymn or chorus associated with the word should start singing it, and we would all join in. We sang acapella, with no musical accompaniment. That proved to be interesting. The bass singers usually started the songs too low, while the sopranos sang too high.

To begin, I shouted out the word FRIEND. Someone in the middle row began singing, "What a friend we have in Jesus, All our sins and griefs to bear." By the second line, we all joined in. At the end of that song, one of the men called out the word GRACE. Of course, Doc crooned, "Amazing grace, how sweet the sound, that saved a wretch like me. I once was lost, but now am found, Was blind, but now I see." We sang four verses of that beloved hymn by heart.

One of the little kids on the front row hollered JESUS. Then the whole group of preschoolers stood up and shouted at the top of their lungs, "Jesus loves me this I know. For the Bible tells me so." It wasn't really singing. No recognizable tune. The rest of the crowd grinned, sat back, and enjoyed the performance. I think the little ones had planned it.

Pee Wee shouted out JOY. All the teens began singing, "I have the joy, joy, joy, joy down in my heart. Where? Down in my heart." This chorus brought back childhood memories, so all joined in singing a rousing rendition. Another yelled the word BIBLE. This time we sang, "The B-I-B-L-E, yes that's the book for me. I stand alone on the Word of God, The B-I-B-L-E."

My husband called out BLOOD and all joined in singing "Power in the Blood." Granny Mae raised her hand and pointed to the hand carved wooden cross behind the pulpit. We reverently sang "The Old Rugged Cross."

When things started slowing down, I told them to peek in their songbooks to find more words. The next word after that was TRUST. Rachel's sweet voice sang, "Tis so sweet to trust in Jesus, Just to take Him at His Word." Pastor Henry hollered VICTORY and began singing "Victory in Jesus" off-key without waiting for anyone else to start it.

We continued this for about fifty minutes. Then a thirty second lull filled the building as folks thought and thumbed through their hymnals. Getting ready to conclude the service with a closing hymn and prayer, I noticed the teenage boys on the back row snickering and jabbing each other in the ribs with their elbows.

Just then, my ornery, mischievous great-nephew shouted out in his changing voice, SEX. I glared at him and wanted to throttle him. His mom slunk down in her seat and covered her face with her hands. The older members gasped. A stunned silence enveloped the whole congregation. After what seemed like an eternity, but probably in all reality was only ten seconds, my ninety-five year old, wheelchair bound mother began singing in her gravely, crackly voice, "Precious Memories, how they linger. How they ever flood my soul." The boys looked as shocked as I felt. Everyone turned and stared at my feisty ninety-five year old mom as she continued. "In the stillness of the midnight, precious, sacred, scenes unfold." When Mom finished singing, the teenagers on the back row started clapping. Soon the whole congregation erupted into a rousing ovation. When things finally calmed down, not knowing what else to do, I asked everyone to stand for the closing prayer.

Honestly, I have to say I've never experienced such an unforgettable church service as that particular 5th Sunday night sing. Maybe it's because I've never tried the word association game again. And I probably never will. Fodder for the old codgers at the general store, that service provided conversation and laughter for days. And of course, they rehash it before every 5th Sunday service.

## STRAIGHT FROM THE COW'S MOUTH
Blake Chambers

Trailing a plume of dust, the stock truck turned off the county road and lurched up the driveway, metal sides clanging noisily as usual. Looking on from his paddock, Lordhorn munched alfalfa and wondered if the truck was dropping off or picking up. Or both.

The morning air was warm and still, reeking of methane and manure. Hordes of flies swarmed in all directions. Later in the day, Lordhorn would have some relief from his constant torment, but for now all he could do was shake his head, flick his tail and stamp his feet. Meanwhile, the arrival of the truck meant he might be pressed into service, so with two quick, well-placed darts of his tongue, Lordhorn cleared dust and alfalfa flakes from each nostril then walked from the hayrack toward the gate at the far end of the paddock where the trucks always parked.

A dark brown Texan Longhorn, ten years old and in the prime of life, Lordhorn was handsome and respected, the unquestioned leader of all the cows who, however briefly, ever spent time in the bovine purgatory otherwise known as the Orion Feedlot. He was stern but fair in his dealing with others and the herd listened to him and obeyed. If they didn't, they were apt to be gored.

Once the truck was in position, the driver got out, slid the ramp into place and opened the doors. Lordhorn counted a dozen tan colored cows of a breed he'd never seen before enter the holding pen and began mooing and trotting nervously about. The last cow to appear on the ramp was a sleek, magnificent heifer. After descending, she spoke quietly and reassuringly to the others – an eloquent Bovine with a trace of a French accent – and within seconds the holding pen was calm again and decidedly quieter. Lordhorn was impressed. This beautiful, tan-colored goddess of a cow was in complete control of the situation, and consequently his services as peacemaker and guide would not be required. The new arrivals were herded by the hired men out of the holding pen through a chute near Lordhorn's paddock and into the pasture where they milled about briefly then settled down to graze. Several Polled Herefords replaced the tan cows in the holding pen and were eventually loaded into the truck, destined, Lordhorn assumed, for the slaughterhouse. As the truck banged and rattled down the dusty gravel driveway, Lordhorn returned to his hayrack and resumed feeding.

Moments later the splendid tan colored heifer approached from behind him and spoke through the bars. "My name is Alaine. What is yours," she said, her accent pleasant and refined, unlike the rough, lowbrow bovine he was accustomed to hearing in and around the lot.

Lordhorn turned and walked toward the attractive, fair-haired stranger. "They call me Lordhorn," he replied.

Alaine stared admiringly at his immense horns, scanning the span from tip to tip. "Impressive," she said. "You're a Longhorn. I've heard of your kind."

"I wish I could say the same for you," said Lordhorn. "I've seen thousands of cows in my day but nothing quite like you. And I mean that in a nice way."

"Thank you," said Alaine. "The feeling is mutual."

"So what b…" Lordhorn began.

"We are Blonde d'Aquitaine. From France."

Lordhorn considered this for a moment before saying, "I see. So that would make you, Alaine d'Aquitaine."

Alaine smiled. "If I had an ear of corn for every time I've heard that one."

"Sorry," Lordhorn replied. "Couldn't resist."

"I forgive you," said Alaine. "You are handsome and sweet, and very polite. I like you, Lordhorn the Longhorn." She lowered her head, glanced briefly at Lordhorn's underside. "A steer," she said. "How disappointing. I think we might have had some fun together."

Staring at the beautiful, sensual creature on the other side of the fence reminded Lordhorn of a time long ago when as a young bull, several heifers at the ranch where he'd been born had joked that his name should actually end in "y." But a few deft strokes of the veterinarian's scalpel had abruptly and forever changed all that. "You're disappointed," he said. "Imagine how I must feel?"

Alaine laughed – a throaty, delicate, enchanting sound – then turned her attention to a car coming up the driveway. The red Chevrolet sedan came to a halt near the entrance to the barn and a fat, bald man got out. Carrying a notebook he immediately employed to try and keep the flies at bay. He waved at Lordhorn, called to him by name, then disappeared into the barn.

"You know him?" asked Alaine.

"Sort of. He was here yesterday. He's actually okay as humans go. A freelance writer, working on a story about beef for some farm journal. Only he calls it an 'ag rag'."

"Charming," Alaine deadpanned.

"Not exactly what you'd call a mainstream journalist," Lordhorn went on. "Told me his next assignment was to research the question 'are clams really happy, and if so why.'" Alaine looked blankly at Lordhorn for a second or two before asking, "This man speaks Bovine?"

"No."

"Then how do you…"

"I speak a modicum of English," Lordhorn replied diffidently. "Most Longhorns do. Not to brag or anything, but we're generally considered to be smarter than other breeds – present company excepted of course." Alaine acknowledged the compliment with a slight nod of her lovely blonde head and Lordhorn resumed, "It's quite rare to find someone like you that I can actually have an intelligent conversation with."

"Tell me about it," Alaine said, rolling her beautiful brown eyes. "So what exactly is your human friend writing about?"

Lordhorn lifted his great rack toward the adjacent pasture. "Them," he said.

Alaine turned and looked behind her. Several black and red cows, heads down, tails swishing, grazed nearby. "Angus?" she said. Lordhorn nodded. Alaine watched as a yearling Angus, only a foot or so away from her, raised its tail and defecated audibly onto the hoof-rutted ground. Mostly liquid, the foul discharge splattered in several directions and an airborne dollop struck Alaine half way up her right foreleg.

"Viral scours," Lordhorn grimaced. "Been a problem around here lately."

Alaine moved away from the offending cow and turned her attention back to Lordhorn. "What could anyone possibly find fascinating about such ill-mannered beasts?"

Lordhorn explained that the fat writer had come to the feedlot to research a story he'd been working on. Tentatively titled, "Why Angus Get All the Love," the feature would, the writer had told Lordhorn the day before, attempt to answer the question whether "Certified Angus Beef" was really superior to other breeds as the media would have everyone believe, or was the phenomenon mostly hype. Lordhorn then went into some detail describing to Alaine how grocery stores and restaurant chains in the United States seemed to glorify Angus more than Herefords for instance or Santa Gertrudis, or Charlois, or even Blonde d'Aquitaine.

"So why all the fanfare?" asked Alaine, frowning at the now elongated greenish brown stain on her foreleg. "It can't be because of their hygienic tendencies."

"They say Angus meat is marbled better than others."

"Marbled," said Alaine. "What does that mean?"

"It's a euphemism for fat."

Alaine thought for moment before replying, "I see. Well the writer should know something about that. He appears quite well-marbled himself."

Lordhorn chuckled approvingly. Not only was this heifer beautiful, she had a sense of humor as well and he found himself silently cursing the terrible finality of the cutting. "I'm told the marbling gives the meat a better flavor," he continued.

"So what do you think?" Alaine asked pointedly. "Is it all hype, or is Angus really better?"

"How should I know," Lordhorn shrugged matter of factly. "I'm vegan like the rest of us. I must say though, grilled meat sure smells good You smell that?" Alaine sniffed the air and wrinkled her nose in disgust. "The owner of the place is putting on a little demonstration for the writer today. Some local school kids are coming to tour the place and participate in a blind taste test over at the pavilion. Angus,

Hereford, Gelbvieh, and I believe Simmental are all featured on the menu."

"Depressing subject," Alaine lamented. "But a fact of life nevertheless."

"Yes," Lordhorn said. "Sooner or later we're all destined for the abattoir."

Alaine shuddered. "A most unpleasant French word."

"Oui," said Lordhorn. "But as you say, a fact of life."

"And death," Alaine added. She looked into Lordhorn's eyes for a few seconds then turned away, watching the many black, brown, red and tan cows grazing, swishing flies and generally lolling about in the pasture. "Look at them," she said. "Poor, stupid creatures. If only they knew the grim reality that awaits." She paused, turned back to Lordhorn and smiled. "Of course if they did they would all stampede for the coast hoping to catch the next freighter to India."

Lordhorn laughed quietly. "You're as quick and literate as you are beautiful," he said, already dreading the moment when inevitably she must depart.

"Thank you," Alaine said, and as if reading his thoughts added, "I shall miss you too."

An awkward silence followed. Finally Alaine sniffed the air again and said, "So tell me, do you think about it often?"

"What? India? Of course. We all do."

"No, no, not that. I mean… ending up on a grill."

"I won't be grilled," Lordhorn said with grave certainty.

"Why not?"

"Longhorn meat is tough and stringy, poorly marbled. At best I'll end up Salisbury steak in one of those Banquet frozen dinners. At worst, dog food. Speaking of which, do you have any idea what a kibble is?"

"None whatsoever," Alaine answered.

"How about a bit?"

"Can't help you there either I'm afraid."

Lordhorn nodded. "Well, thanks anyway. I'll ask the fat writer when he comes round again after the taste test. Maybe he knows."

"So let me get this straight," Alaine said. "He's writing a story about which breed of cow is better marbled?"

Lordhorn nodded. "In essence, yes."

"Sounds terribly boring."

"Interestingly enough, he had the same concern," Longhorn replied. "So he's going to jazz it up, write it from our point of view, anthropomorphize it he said."

Alaine pondered this for a moment. "Interesting word," she said. "What does it mean?"

"It means to ascribe human characteristics to animals or other objects. For example, most humans think cows can't talk but in the guy's story they..."

"What? Cows can't talk!" Alaine said, feigning disbelief, her lovely brown eyes twinkling. "We seem to be doing a fair job of it wouldn't you say?"

"Yeah," Lordhorn said, "Little do they know, huh? Anyway, after the contest is over today he's going to come talk to me and announce his findings. I'll discuss it with another cow, presumably you, and that's how his readers will know which breed won."

In the distance a school bus turned into the driveway and lumbered toward the barn, a great cloud of gravel dust spewing from behind. "Looks like the kids are here," Lordhorn said. "Show time. I'll see ya round."

"See you 'round? " Alaine said, puzzled.

"It's a colloquialism," said Lordhorn. "Like see ya later. It means we will meet again."

"I hope so," Alaine replied.

Anticipating his handler's arrival, Lordhorn apologized to Alaine for having to cut their visit short, then walked toward the gate of his paddock and waited. Alaine, maintaining a safe distance from the young loose-bowelled Angus, strolled out to the pasture. As she moved away, Lordhorn heard her practicing, "See ya 'round. See ya later. See ya 'round. See ya...."

Two teachers and several students from the Orion High School Home Economics class climbed out of the bus and were ushered by the owner of the feedlot to a nearby pavilion. A hired man entered Lordhorn's paddock, brushed him clean, polished his horns, sprayed him with fly repellant, buckled a halter onto his head and led him outside toward the gathering of noisy newcomers. The smell of grilled beef intensified. Yes, Lordhorn thought, perverse as it may seem, the smell was really quite delightful. As he and his handler neared the pavilion Lordhorn could see smoke rising and burgers sizzling on an enormous black grill.

The owner welcomed the students and the teacher, said lunch would be served in a few minutes, and encouraged them to have their pictures taken with Lordhorn while they waited for the burgers to finish cooking. Lordhorn was used to this sort of thing of course and happily accepted his role as mascot and public relations liaison for the feedlot. As long as he remained useful in this manner he could delay the inevitable confrontation with the captive bolt stun gun.

While he graciously posed for pictures and ate an assortment of treats – range cubes, carrot slices, molasses infused corn pellets – out of the palms of several giddy highschoolers, Lordhorn had to admit that compared to most residents of the feedlot, his life was pretty good. Before and during all events such as this one he was cleaned, sprayed, fed, and generally fussed over. For a cow, he had it made. As he looked back on his life, his only real regret was the cutting of course but that had been years ago. Since then he'd adapted to life as a steer and parlayed his innate intelligence and docility into what turned out to be a most agreeable gig. As long as his massive horns remained in place and continued to impress the occasional visitors, his position was secure. He would remain Lord of his realm.

The photo op ended after several minutes and Lordhorn was returned to his paddock. As the handler removed his halter, Lordhorn could hear the students in the pavilion laughing and squealing with delight as they were blindfolded and asked to sample multiple burgers from the giant grill. When the festivities ended an hour or so later, the owner came by Lordhorn's paddock, spoke kindly to him, brushed him, rubbed his forehead and gave him an extra scoop of grain in appreciation of his performance.

After he finished eating, Lordhorn looked through the bars of his paddock and pondered the other cows scattered throughout the pasture: the smug, indifferent Angus, so full of themselves and their press clippings; the polled Herefords, a once proud and prominent breed, now under-appreciated, often bullied and taunted by the pompous, overbearing Angus; and the newly arrived foreigners, the Blonde d'Aquitaine. The mere thought of the stately and beautiful Alaine caused a faint stirring in his underside, a sensation he'd not felt in years, and even though he could no longer act on it, he was nonetheless grateful for it.

The next morning a truck arrived and backed up to the holding pen. A light rain had fallen during the night so there was no dust for a change. The truck driver and the hired men leaned against the rails smoking cigarettes, chatting about baseball and women until at length Lordhorn heard one of them say, "Time to get a move on boys. Boss says to round up the all frenchies. That new burger joint in town bought the lot of 'em." The truck driver smoked, drank coffee from a thermos, and talked on a cell phone, as the hired men retreated into the barn to saddle their horses. Lordhorn tried to eat some alfalfa but it tasted sour.

When Alaine wandered in from the pasture and stopped at Lordhorn's paddock a few minutes later, Lordhorn pretended nothing was wrong, an act that out of necessity he'd perfected over many years. "Well?" Alaine said.

"Well what?" Lordhorn responded.

Alaine rolled her enormous brown eyes. "Who won?" she asked.

"Oh yes, that," said Lordhorn. "Well, from what I understand, the outcome was inconclusive. As promised, the writer came by after it was over yesterday and said the results were all over the place. As many of the school kids preferred Gelbvieh as Angus. The writer did too for that matter. Hereford and Simmental wound up tied. Anyway, he's going to report that in his opinion at least, the whole Angus is better campaign is mostly hype. Then it's off to New England to begin work on the clam piece."

"I'm glad," Alaine said. "I had the misfortune of spending time last night with several Angus. To a cow I found them haughty and tiresome, dazzled by their own press clippings I think. Perhaps the well-marbled writer's story will take them down a notch or two. It would serve them right. Of course I can't say I care much for Gelbvieh either. They aren't as disagreeable as Angus but they're not far behind. They're German, you know, brawny and indelicate, stubborn, humorless."

Lordhorn had had encountered his share of Gelbvieh during his time at the lot and found himself agreeing wholeheartedly with everything Alaine had said about them. "Glorified cart pullers," he added with a sardonic grin.

As Alaine laughed her joyous, seductive laugh, Lordhorn heard a commotion behind him, turned and looked out at the pasture. Alaine's many tan colored companions trotted toward the paddock, herded by two men on horseback and the owner's new dog, an irksome, dung-obsessed, six month old border collie named Stupefy. Already in a foul mood, Lornhorn thought to himself, the little flea bag better keep his distance today.

"Breakfast," Alaine said happily as her companions arrived, then turned and walked out to meet them. Over her shoulder she called out to Lordhorn in a precise American accent, "See ya 'round."

Lordhorn suppressed a tear, turned and halfheartedly pulled a mouthful of alfalfa from the hayrack. It tasted even sourer than before.

Compiled By: Roy L. Wachter

# CONSCIENCE
## C. B. Buckley

One day I had to solve two problems as a child. I did not have a quarter to buy a milkshake. Also, I lacked permission to cross the road from my house to the local drugstore.

Visions of a delicious chocolate milkshake danced through my head. I had to have it. My nervous fingers found a quarter in my mother's purse. I looked over my shoulder as I crossed the forbidden road and raced to the nearby drug store.

I saw my image in the mirror as I climbed up on a stool. My fingers rubbed across the sparkling clean marble counter. Behind the counter a thin man whistled and placed a silver cylinder into a metal device that made the most wonderful whirling sound. Then he poured the delicious ice cream concoction into a sparkling glass. Who could resist this dessert?

I gained the attention of the thin man in the black-striped shirt and the red arm band. He snorted through a bicycle mustache. "What can I get you, kiddo?"

I plunked down the stolen quarter and snorted back, "A chocolate milk shake with those cookies!"

"Those cookies are wafers. Coming right up, sonny!"

As I drank through the straw, ate lumps of ice cream, and nibbled on the wafers, my eyes kept returning to the huge mirror.

"I should not have stolen from my mother who has been nothing but good to me." The image in the mirror was of a thief. I finished my shake, walked out, and regurgitated. Guilt pushed me home and placed me in front of my mother. "I am sorry." "I won't ever cross that road again." "I'll never steal again." My mother was not one who said, "Wait till Dad gets home!"

Instead her discipline was swift. She lectured about the dangers of crossing the road alone, followed by a reminder of the "Thou shall not steal" commandment, and concluded with a switch to my legs.

I welcomed Dad's arrival as a buffer between mother and me. Besides, it was her purse that I had invaded - not his billfold. Perhaps, he would not take it as personal as her. I was wrong.

Dad had a salient way of behavior modification: He raged, "We are certainly disappointed in you. You will stay in this yard, do you understand? A bus about killed your dog. What do you think that a bus or car on the highway could do to you? I will not be known as the man who raised a thief. Do you understand? Think about this, young man! What gives you the right to take another's money or property! How would you feel if someone took your bike? You would probably want them arrested and put in jail, right."

Later, my mother disciplined, "I think that you learned today why it is wrong to disobey and to steal. I was proud that you had the courage to come to me and to tell me how you had wronged me, but let's never do this again. Promise me that you will never cross that road or steal."

I did promise. More importantly, I never broke my promise. In fact, I found honesty as the keystone of sportsmanship. I would never win a tennis match by cheating my opponent on line calls. Why should I steal his points by cheating? I would not like to be treated that way. If I cheated and stole an opponent's important point, it would bother me as much as stealing a quarter from my mother's purse as a kid. And, believe me, I was not a perfect child, but my parents took the time to discipline me; it has made all the difference in the world.

## MURDER IN MEETING ROOM THREE
### Molly Daniels

Tara gritted her teeth. If the moderator of the group didn't monopolize the conversation, maybe some of her ideas could be voted upon. Shifting in her seat, she tried to focus on what topic they had veered from.

"Okay, now what were we talking about again? Oh yes, the deadline for critiquing each other's stories. Mine is finished, and Kim has already told me how brilliant it is, so everyone try to have yours finished by next week, okay?" Rita's nasal whine sent shivers down Tara's spine. Why she had agreed to be here was beyond imaginable.

"You're a good writer," her teacher had told her. "This group will give you further encouragement, more than I can give you, and your potential will grow."

Believing her, Tara had joined the local group, only to discover at the last meeting, most of the members to be self-absorbed, spoiled brats who thought any words they put on paper were next to holy and should never be changed.

Anyone with a fifth grade education can see sentences need both a subject and a verb, Tara seethed. Rita just likes to flaunt the fact her mom writes for the newspaper and one of her stories was published on the kiddie page.

"Tara? Do you have anything to add?" With a start, Tara realized all six were staring at her.

"Uh, I'm sorry, my mind must have wandered. What was the question?"

Rita's pretty face twisted into a scowl. "Kim said your story on Google Docs wasn't quite finished. Will you have it ready by next week? She also said— "I said the plot looked a bit weak. Maybe we should schedule you for the next one?"

Tara sat up straight and took a deep breath. "I have it finished in longhand and will post it to the site tomorrow. It says that at the bottom, Kim."

Kim giggled. "Oh, I thought that was what your character said. My bad."

Tara flinched. Of all the slang terms lately, "my bad" was the one she couldn't stand.

"Meeting adjourned then. See you all next week. Tara, the purpose of putting our work on Google Docs is so everyone can read them in time for the meetings. If you don't have your work up, then how can we critique it?"

"I do my best work in study hall, and last week my computer lit teacher refused to let me copy my stuff on the site. I just haven't gotten around to it. I promise I'll have it up tonight."

"See that you do." With a flounce, Rita started for the door.

All at once, an alarm sounded and the lights went out. Tara, who had just stood up, felt for the chair and sat back down among the screams. The girls called to each other, finding their ways back to the table or pulling out their cell phones to illuminate their way.

"Where's Rita?" Kim's frantic voice rose in pitch. "I can't find her."

"I can't open the door," came another voice. "It must be tied into the alarm system."

The lights flickered back on, and Tara stood up to stuff her notebook back into her backpack.

Kim screamed. "Rita!"

Tara turned with the others. Rita's body lay prone in front of the door, blood seeping from her ear.

"Oh, my God!"

"Somebody call 9-1-1!"

"Who would do such a thing?"

Tara jumped onto her chair, stuck two fingers in her mouth, and blew an ear-piercing whistle. "Quiet!"

Five sets of startled eyes looked at her.

"Has anyone called 9-1-1?"

Blonde-haired Lisa raised her hand. "I-I was just about to hit the "send" button.

Tara nodded. "Okay. Go ahead. Secondly, did the door ever open?"

"N-no," Kim sniffed, cradling Rita's head. "Maybe… it all happened so fast!"

"Then can someone try to open it?" Impatience seeped into her voice as she stepped back onto the floor. Leaving her backpack on the table, Tara stopped red-haired Susan, who was near the door. "Don't use your bare hands. Use your shirt, in case the police are able to find fingerprints."

"Good idea." Susan pulled the tail of her shirt from her jeans and twisted the knob. The door opened without any issues.

"Everyone stay put until the police arrive." Tara clapped her hand over her mouth as she walked toward Rita's body, the trickle of blood pooling near her head. "Who could have done this? I just met her last week…. did she have any enemies?"

"Who the hell left you in charge?" Kim snarled. "My best friend is dead and you don't seem to care!"

The sound of sirens wailed in the background. Lisa closed her phone and moved toward Kim. "They'll be here soon. Was anyone else involved? Should we check the library? What if the librarian is dead, too? What if we're the only ones left?" She drew in a breath and the color drained from her face. "What if he comes back for us?" She screamed and whirled around, right into Leslie's arms. "Let me go! I don't want to die!"

"Lisa! Snap out of it." Leslie, who had been the only one genuinely interested in what Tara had to contribute to the earlier discussion, shook the younger girl, then slapped her across the face. "Not to sound like a cliché, but pull yourself together. This is no time to fall apart." She held the sobbing freshman in her arms.

Tara blinked, then turned back to Kim. "My uncle's a detective, and I love listening to his stories. One of the first things they always do is dust for prints. Don't you watch any crime dramas?"

Kim blanched. "I like Real Housewives and Pretty Little Liars. Why would I want to watch something that morbid?"

Indeed. Remember who you're talking to. Tara gritted her teeth and mentally counted to ten. "Susan, step out into the library and see if you see anyone."

"What if they kill me next?" The young girl's eyes were wide with fear.

"Oh please. If they were going to kill you, they would have done it the minute you opened the door. Don't be such a dweeb." Kim dissolved into tears again.

"Over here!" Tara heard Lisa call. "The police are here."

The harried librarian entered, then stopped short at the sight before her. Behind her, Susan held open the door as the two policemen entered, calmly ushering the older woman aside. One knelt at the body while the other spoke into his microphone.

"Can anyone tell me what happened?"

Kim's wails grew loud as she spoke to the first officer. Leslie spoke up to the second and gave her account. The others agreed.

"We don't know why the lights flashed off, or why we couldn't open the door."

The librarian covered her mouth. "That's because it's a safety precaution. It isolates this room from the others. We really don't know why. That's why I tried to discourage your group from meeting here." She knelt beside Kim, her arm around the girl's shoulders. "Rita liked the fact it was quiet back here. Come, sweetie… let the officers do their job."

"But she's my best friend. I don't want to leave her." Kim sobbed.

The first policeman took over. "I understand. But we need to move you girls to a different location so we can do our job." He stood up. "What would be very helpful is if you would all go into the other room and write your statements for me, while it is fresh in your mind. Mrs. Hippensteele will provide you with pens and paper if you have none."

Tara collected her backpack and followed the others. As she passed the policeman, she scowled. "This isn't the way my uncle described it. You haven't even dusted the doorknob for fingerprints yet."

"Our first objective is to clear the crime scene." The second officer smiled. "I appreciate your cooperation, but not all crime scenes are treated the same."

Tara sighed and took a seat at the table beside Leslie. "Can I open my laptop and write it that way?"

"They want us to write it in longhand, so they can collect it," Leslie explained, and passed her several sheets of paper. "The sooner we write it, the sooner they'll let us return home."

Tara tapped her pen against her teeth, then began writing.

Several minutes passed. Satisfied with the way she'd written the events, Tara put down her paper. "That's weird. Where are Rita's parents? The coroner? Shouldn't an ambulance be outside yet?"

"They've already taken Rita to the hospital." Mrs. Hippensteele gathered the statements. "They took her out through the emergency exit at the back of the room, so as not disturb the other patrons."

"What other patrons?" Tara frowned, looking around at the near-deserted library. A sudden fear struck her. What if the killer were still in here? What if Mrs. Hippensteele was the killer? Was she planning to kill all of them?

Stop it. You're as bad as Lisa. Tara tried to calm her rising panic and forced herself to stand. "So we are free to go now? Should we go to the hospital and offer our condolences to Rita's family?"

"That won't be necessary." Mrs. Hippensteele ushered the girls toward the front door. "I'm sure there will be a memorial tomorrow at school, with counselors for you girls to speak to."

"I'm not going to school tomorrow." Kim wiped her cheeks with the soggy hem of her shirt. "Rita and I had every class together. It just won't be the same without her there."

Tara walked home, a knot forming in her stomach. True, she hadn't known Rita very well, and though she found the girl to be a complete airhead, she was sorry for the brutal death. *I hope Kim and the others will be okay.*

When Tara arrived at school the next day, she noticed something strange. She couldn't figure out what felt out of place, but during the passing period after first period, it hit her. No one had mentioned anything about Rita's murder! There had been no announcement, no one gossiping, no speculation.

Tara reversed course and went to the office to speak with the principal.

"Why hasn't there been any mention of Rita Wilcox?" She stood in the doorway with her books clutched to her chest. "I know I don't have any classes with her, since she's a senior, but still.... shouldn't have an announcement been made?"

The principal stood up. "You weren't on the list of names I was given. I'm sorry, Tara. When do you have English class?"

Huh? "What does my English class have to do with it? A girl has died, and all you have to say is 'when is my English class'?" Confusion turned to anger. "I know she was a royal bitch, but her memory deserves better." She turned to go.

"Tara, wait." A hand landed on her shoulder. "We called the others in to explain. Apparently your name was left off the list, so my sincere apologies. Trust me when I say everything will be explained at your next English class."

The bell rang. "I'm supposed to be there now." Tara shuffled her books. "I guess I'll be needing a pass."

"Just a moment." Going to his desk, the principal activated the intercom and told Tara's teacher she was on her way and to hold the lesson. "Okay, you can go now."

Thoroughly confused, Tara rushed to her classroom and took her seat, detecting an air of anticipation in the room. Nobody questioned her about her trip to the office, nor did anyone look at her. What the hell was going on?

Her teacher cleared her throat. "Perception" was written on the Smartboard. "Your homework assignment has been granted an extension. You now have til tomorrow to hand it in." A few of Tara's classmate's cheered. "Yes, yes, I know." She walked around her desk to lean against it. "We talked yesterday about point of view, and how important it was to write a story from different points of view. To illustrate how everyone's perception of an event can be different, we staged an experiment yesterday." She walked over to the door and looked out into the hallway, then beckoned. To Tara's surprise, Rita, Kim, and Leslie entered. "Tara, can you come up here, please?"

Trembling, Tara stood up and felt her eyes fill with tears. "You're alive? Am I dreaming?"

Rita smiled in a smug way. "I didn't think you cared, since you were so cold about it last night."

"I thought everyone had lost their minds!" Tara clenched her fists. "Someone had to take control." She swiped at the tears trickling down her cheeks.

"Girls, girls…I admit, this was a little unorthodox, but actually it was Rita's idea. Read your story, Tara." Handing the paper to her, the teacher smiled and whispered in her ear.

Composing herself, Tara looked up at the praise coming from her adored English teacher. "Really?" She sniffed, then began to read her account.

"Very good. Kim, read yours, please."

Astonished, Tara and the rest of the class listened as Kim read hers, describing in detail Rita's lifeless body, but no mention of anything else, except for Tara's bossy attitude. Leslie's was next, and while hers was similar to Tara's, her version praised Tara's ability to keep her head. Lisa's outburst had been exaggerated, while Tara's was more accurate.

When finished, a question-and-answer session followed, then the students were given a study period. Tara was told to get her books, then follow Rita, Kim, and Leslie to the other classes.

"Was everyone in on it?" She asked Leslie, still not trusting herself near Rita.

"Yes. Mrs. Hippensteele approved it, and her son, who was the policeman who checked Rita's body, had been alerted in advance of the call coming in."

"But the blood…"

"Food coloring." Leslie tucked her arm through Tara's. "This is a story which will go down in Orion High School history."

Compiled By: Roy L. Wachter

## ASTON OAKES
### Amy Gardner

This story is about a ghost house in Orion, Indiana. Let's go back to the 1800's. John Aston Warder, a doctor and first president of the American Forestry Association purchased a 300 acre plot from President Benjamin Harrison. Yes, President Harrison! In 1875, Warder built a 21-room creek rock structure. Yes, 21 rooms!

My husband lived at this location in the 1970's and I'm sure he had seen and heard many ghostly things, but he didn't mention them. Besides, I didn't believe in a ghost. Although I had heard numerous ghost stories, to me, "ghost stories" were only stories.

Believe me, it didn't take me long to become a believer in ghosts. My husband was a caretaker of the property and I assisted as a guide by taking people through the home and telling its history.

The first strange thing I noticed occurred on a cold winter morning. Carl had gone to work leaving a small dog whom sitting on the couch by me. Suddenly, I heard someone going up the stairs followed by heavy footsteps in the rooms overhead. There was nobody in the building except me and the dog!

I got up from the couch, slowly walked out into the foyer and stood there motionless. I heard one of the recessed doors on the second floor open and close. Slowly I walked up the stairs. When I got to the second floor, an old fashioned rocking chair was rocking. I stepped onto the second floor. The chair stopped rocking.

Since my husband was a builder, he asked my brother Phil to work with him. Phil stayed on our second floor. I didn't mention my experiences with the ghost, but after staying one night at our place, Phil came down for breakfast and said, "Amy, were you upstairs around two this morning moving furniture?" I said, "No, I don't move furniture in the daytime much less at night!" Phil gave me a quick glance, rolled his eyes and exclaimed, "I'll stay up there one more night, but if strange things move around, I'm getting out of there!" He did stay in the front room on the second floor the following night and the next morning, had quite a story to tell. He had observed a misty, ghost-like figure of a woman in a thin gown floating through the window. She had perched on the bottom of his bed.

I had to grin as I thought perhaps this was wishful thinking. After all, Phil was a handsome young fellow and could have possibly had a dream. He declared, "This was no dream! I will no longer sleep in that front room. Perhaps I'll move to the other side of the hall." His new room had a fireplace, a large closet and two large windows.

As far as I know, Phil had no experiences in this room, but something unusual happened when I needed the overhead light on, it would always go off. I finally had to command, "I want the light left on!" It stayed on. I just had to talk to them in a firm manner.

I went to Lexington's V.A. Hospital to visit my uncle. When I got back home, I noticed quite a lot of blood on the floor in the living room. My husband had accidents quite often, so I thought he had injured himself. He looked up from his paper and said, "I didn't have an accident. It's not my blood."

I shook my head in disbelief and went into the kitchen to get a bucket of water and soap to clean up the mess. I looked overhead. Small drops of dried blood came from the ceiling. Carl went up to the room above, removed some planks and there was no sign of blood, or any animal that could have shed blood. He put the flooring back down and the mystery was never solved.

The next morning Carl left around seven for work, but I heard his truck racing back up the long winding driveway. He rushed into the house and asked me to call the police. A car inside the entrance of the property was on fire. The police and fire trucks arrived quickly. A policeman walked over near the car and yelled, "There's a body inside this burning car!"

This is what had happened. A couple intended to go to a drag race in the area but decided to do a little dope and have sex on the property. Amazingly, the young man admitted he had killed the girl after she told him she had HIV. I never did hear anything further on that case.

The teachers at the area school heard about the spirits at the Aston mansion and asked if they could bring sleeping bags and spend a night. Of course, I was agreeable. Since they were determined to have an experience, I told some of the girls that I would put an object into the dumb waiter elevator that would howl like a ghost when the wind blew. The old maid in the group wasn't told.

During the night, the wind picked up and the "ghost" went wild. The old maid leaped to her feet and woke up all the others so they could hear this strange thing. As far as I know, there wasn't any ghost activity that night.

My daughter, Eva, came to visit and brought her ten-year-old daughter, Julie. While riding her bicycle near a lake below the house, Julie heard a voice calling her name. She came to the house and said, "Mom, what did you want? You yelled my name twice." I said, "I didn't call you!" Julie insisted, "I heard the voice too when I road my bike too close to the lake."

I hadn't told Eva about any ghost activities because I didn't want her to worry or be afraid while visiting The Aston. However, after she was left alone while the rest of us went to the grocery, she heard footsteps in the foyer and on the stairs. She went into the hall and yelled, "Is anybody here?" No one was in the building. She was in the home alone.

When Eva went back to Michigan, she told her husband, Rick that there were strange footsteps heard at The Aston. He said, "Oh sure. Tell me another one!"

The next time they visited, Rick came along. He and Eva stayed in the front bedroom on the first floor. During the night, Rick decided to have a cigarette. He wandered out into the hall leading to the foyer. The bright moon was seen shining through the huge window illuminating the bend of the Ohio River. Suddenly, as he walked down the hall in semi-darkness, he heard footsteps like a woman in high heels coming toward him.

He raced back to Eva and said, "Eva, there's footsteps out there!"

Eva said, "Well, what did I tell you!" He became a believer.

During rainstorms, I always had to climb the stairs to the third floor and place a large barrel under where the tile roofing was missing. To keep the rain from ruining the beautiful wood floors, I had the job of dipping a large bucket into the barrel and throwing water out the window. I remember times when the electricity went off as I climbed those stairs as the lightning struck and briefly lit my way. It was a good thing that I was seldom afraid.

A large metal container existed on the other side of a trap door on the third floor, perhaps eight foot by eight foot and three feet high, whose purpose was to catch rainwater. The water was piped to the rooms below providing a running water system. This mansion highlighted bathrooms with toilets that flushed. It had servant quarters, wine cellar and basement stoves with everything to prepare meals. The shower was on the outside of the building at the basement entrance. (I'm sure nobody ever peeked from the woods below.)

When the property was sold to a developer, the day papers were signed, and all through that night I heard what seemed like at least forty people of all ages crying. This went on for hours. I'd get up, turn on lights, brew tea and then when I'd finally would go back to bed...more sobbing. After waking Carl up, I asked him if he'd heard anything. He replied, "No, I haven't heard a thing!"

We moved out of The Aston shortly afterwards leaving the "congregational crying" as the last ghost activity that I remember.

A young man bought the home from the developer. I heard he was quite happy with his purchase. He's made repairs and the home is a magnificent sight to behold. He told me shortly after he bought the home that I could visit any time, but to date I haven't done that. I'd like to ask him if he's ever heard anything, but maybe I'll just leave well enough alone.

## THE MOUSE HOUSE
### Georgia Prewett Buckley

Poppa Mouse pulled the soft fuzz back from Momma Mouse's nest and looked at his new little baby mice: totally bald, pink, squeaking. He burst with pride. Poppa gave Momma loving looks of appreciation.

Suddenly, a loud noise...a big boom! The air filled quickly with dust and dirt. The floor shook under their mice feet. Instantly, Poppa and Momma pulled the little nest of babies out of the house through a crack in the foundation. All squinted as they looked into the bright sunshine, but saw a very large machine with a big ball attached to a chain, swinging madly at their home! Walls and windows came shattering down climaxing in a deafening noise.

The little mice knew they had to do something fast to save their lives. They saw garbage cans and a pile of boxes sitting by the sidewalk across the street, awaiting pick-up. Poppa turned the babies out of the nest. While Momma watched them, he tugged and pushed the little nest across the street and up and under a cardboard box. Then he ran back and took each precious baby, one by one, across the street gently placing the newborn back into the nest. When the last one was placed, Momma Mouse climbed in to comfort the upset babies.

Although the mice parents could clearly see what was going on, they were shocked to see their generational home being destroyed, although not surprised. Other mouse families had the same thing happen to them. Town people did not care about old houses and the history they could tell. Beautiful old homes had been torn down all over town. These historical structures were replaced with parking or bare lots...the town now resembled a snaggle-toothed old crone. The beauty of the town destroyed, one lovely old home at a time. Every home-demolition-project meant that more dislodged mice had to find new homes.

Most of the time the displaced mice were not welcomed, especially when they came with their children, aunts, uncles, and grandparents. Close-knit mice families do not want intruders. The little mice family that once lived at 1017 E. Main Street knew they would have a difficult time finding a new home.

Mice tell each generation all about their history; therefore, both parents knew the history of their home built in the late 1800's by the B&O Railroad Company for company men and their families to live in. There were six houses in a row, identically built, except this first built house had a unique feature a special little room at the end of the entry hall where workers came on payday to pay for their insurance. This feature left the kitchen smaller than the other five houses, although it was plenty big for a large wood-and-coal cook-stove, a Hoosier kitchen cabinet, table and chairs, and a sink.

A big arched doorway dominated the entry hallway leading into the living room featuring a beautiful fireplace with a coal grate surrounded with glazed tile, a tile hearth, and an ornately carved mantel. Leading off that room into the dining room were nine-feet-tall pocket doors that went into the walls, when not in use. One could walk through a small butler's pantry and into the kitchen. A door from the other side of the kitchen led into the insurance room. All of the rooms led to each other so the little mice could run in a big circle before finding a hole to get back into the basement, should the cat be after them.

The hand-carved winding stairway ascended to the upstairs where the mice scampered playfully between the four bedrooms and the bathroom. The young mice delighted in climbing the stairs and sliding down the banister; it was so much fun! When the folks were all asleep, the mice played hide and seek among the canned goods in the pantry. They always found crumbs and food left out for a midnight snack. The only evidence left behind showing their partying were their little droppings.

Every lady of the house hated and pledged war against the mice. Besides traps, some women put out poison bait which fooled many little mice. The death rate became alarming! Then the mice wised up and learned what foods to avoid. In the meantime there were many mice funerals.

The story is told about Aunt Lucy and Uncle Ray both meeting their doom in one raid on the kitchen. There, under the sink, was a delicious looking bowl of sweet-smelling food. Both Auntie and Uncle were very hungry. They made gluttons of themselves! Shortly, they both developed they both developed a terrible stomach ache and soon departed their world.

The whole mouse family came together and had a double funeral with both bodies placed in a Diamond match box, lined with cotton pulled from a hole in a living room couch. The teenagers with sharper teeth worked quicker than the older mice with dull teeth from all the mouse holes that they had made over the years.

There was a mouse meeting to decide what method of disposal for the bodies. Since it was winter, there was deep snow. Burial was out of the question. The only thing left was a dignified cremation. The oldest male mouse Grandad Pop Pop, with fur that had turned a pale gray, nearly white. He gave an excellent sermon based on his wisdom. A mouse quartet sung many favorite songs.

When the last family member went by the match box and said their farewells, the eight strongest mice awaited to shove the matchbox coffin into the coal grate. The man of the house, unaware of the funeral and cremation, made a big fire to last all night. After the master of the house slowly plodded up the stairs, the little mice waited until they heard loud snoring coming from every bedroom and then emerged quickly from behind the large bookcase.

Each pallbearer mouse had his little front paw hooked in a hole gnawed in the match box. In union they are heaved with all of their might. The matchbox went flying the hardwood floor and the tile hearth! With a final thrust the matchbox went under the grate! With one big whoof of fire it was gone. All the mice turned their backs and shed many tears as they returned to their little apartments.

Sometimes it was hard not to be tricked into taking food off of a trap. Poppa's father told of the time his Uncle Joe went up to find something to eat and did not return home. Poppa searched for him. He found him strangled by a wire trap. He had not even got a bite of the cheese! His eyes bulged out with a wire across his neck. Poppa pulled and pulled, but there was no way to release Uncle Joe from the trap. Later he was horrified to see the lady of the house flip poor Uncle Joe out the back door. The big cat caught him in mid air. Poppa did not stay around to see the end of this grizzly scene. Later, the whole mouse family held a memorial for poor Uncle Joe.

When the city was founded, a big sewer was built going from one end of the town to the other end. This sewer ran through the backyard and was about five feet high and made totally of brick. Twenty years ago a big hole appeared in the backyard. Huge sewer rats came out at night, frolicking in the moonlight. The lady of the house called the city sewer department who poured a truck load of gravel down the hole. The sewer department created a large seepage bed causing the basement to fill with water up to the floor joists. The homeowners had a constant battle, especially keeping the sump pump going. When the basement water was tested, it contained E. Coli from the sewer.

All the young mice were warned not to go near the water and, by all means, not to drink it. The city refused to admit that the sewer was leaking because it would cost too much money to repair a nearly-one-hundred-years-old sewer.

A narrow sidewalk led from the backdoor to the coal house. A sidewalk also went around the house. When this house was originally built before the invention of the automobile, the constant clicking sound of horses and carriages was very pleasant. Ancestors of the mice loved the slow pace of the city. Mice grandparents repeated many stories about the people in the old house. The main entertainment for the little mice was listening to the older mice tell stories about previous human residents of the house. They also liked to listen to the humans above them. There was always something going on and they were never bored.

The first family that lived in the house had two beautiful girls and a boy. There were three ballrooms and these girls never lacked for an escort to a dance. The livery stable was located on the hill south of the town. When the boys called on the girls, they came in a rented carriage. The girls carried their ballroom slippers in a fancy bag equipped with a drawstring convenient for the girl to loop over her arm. As soon as the girls arrived at the dance, they changed their shoes. This practice kept their dancing shoes clean from the street dirt and the horse manure. Mice history told of the boys dressed in tuxedos and the girls in flowing ballroom gowns dancing the night away.

The mice also watched the girls, donned in long white dresses, carrying a lace parasol, leaving the house to go to the park on a Sunday afternoon. There they would stroll with their boyfriends. It was an age of glamour and beauty.

The railroad tracks were in the back of their house. When the big steam engines came roaring down the track, huffing and puffing black smoke, it shook the house. Nearly every year someone had to climb up on the slate roof and carefully seal the chimney, where it had broken loose and let rain in. Surprisingly, the slate roof lasted the entire time the house did.

The mice families were so used to the train that they did not notice it and and slept right through the rumbling and shaking.
Sometime during the 1950s, the trains were changed to diesel and there was no longer black soot all over the house. They could hear the people upstairs being so thankful.

Sometimes the train would stop on the tracks. None of the mice would go outside for fear of the big cat that held guard at the back door. There is always a dare devil teenager in every family and in this mouse family it was Ralph the Renegade. He was always looking for someone to make a dare with him, just to show how brave he was. This particular day all of his friends prodded him to go outside, across the back yard, and climb up on the stopped train. Ralph peeked out the hole in the foundation and saw that the big cat was nowhere in sight. He made a mad dash across the back yard, scurried up the weeping willow tree, and climbed up on the back platform of the stopped train. Just about this time the train started up and poor Ralph had no way to get off. What a ride he took.

By the time the train approached Wheatland, it was going at such a high rate of speed that Ralph could hardly hold on to the step. Finally, with much effort, he got on the platform and quickly went inside when the conductor came out to have a smoke. No one on the train was expecting a mouse and he went unnoticed. The passengers were eating and drinking out of picnic baskets. They dropped crumbs on the floor. What a feast Ralph had. The train was swaying back and forth. Ralph became very sleepy so he settled into the corner under the back seat and went sound asleep. When he woke up, he realized the train had stopped and all was quiet. Just about this time he heard the sweeping sound of a big broom and shortly he saw it poking under each seat. He managed to get into the corner and out of the way. Then the people started coming in and Ralph knew not to move.

Soon the conductor came through the car announcing Olney, Illinois. The mouse knew it would not be long until they stopped at his home. It was not long before the conductor came by telling everyone that the next stop would be where Ralph would get off. With much squealing of the brakes and puffing of the engine, the train stopped . Ralph jumped off and headed east along the tracks. It was a long ten blocks. By the time he got home it was dark. He was so tired he could hardly crawl through the hole and back to his family home. Since mice sleep in the daytime and nights are their waking time, all the family was up and when he came in. Oh, how joyful they were! Everyone wanted to hear about his big experience. All the teenagers were in great awe and had him repeat over and over what had happened. So Ralph was known from then on as Ralph the Brave."

After watching their home being torn down and knowing that they could not live under the cardboard box for long, the parents decided to look for a new home. Mice children are not like people children and can be left alone because they always mind their parents. When they were told to be very quiet, they obeyed. Poppa and Momma went out to scout for a new home. A restaurant was across the street. The mice parents knew there would be lots of food, but when they went around the place there was no way to gain entry. After that defeat, they went up the street, always looking over their shoulder for a cat.

There was one house left of the original six houses. They hurriedly crossed the street. Being the wee hours of the morning, there were no buggies or carriages in sight. The mice quickly gained entry. Since the house was exactly like their old home, they knew their way around. How happy they were! They realized they had found the perfect house.

By this time the little mice could toddle along, but it did take a long time to get them to cover one block. This time they decided to make residence in the couch instead of the basement. Before long they had gnawed out an apartment in the stuffing of the back of the couch.

Momma mouse called a family meeting and explained, "We are the first mice to occupy this home. We should be very quiet and should never leave any evidence that we live here."

The new rules declared that all mice should run to the basement for bathroom calls and never leave teeth marks on any boxes of food.

Mr. and Mrs. Forrester were the owners of this house. They were the loving parents of twelve children. Oh, what a happy family this was! Mr. Forrester was a piano tuner, and the mice loved to hear the ping...ping of his work. Since both parents and the children were beautiful singers, music filled the house nearly all the time.

All the Forrest children left home to make their way in the world but came back frequently. One day some of the girls came back and sang, the National Anthem, which they had sung at a Colts game in Indianapolis. Even when alone, Mr. and Mrs. Forrester would sing. Oh, how the little mice loved to hear them harmonize! Joy and happiness surrounded them at all times. All the mice agreed that sometimes a cloud has a silver lining. Their happiness was now complete in their new home.

Compiled By: Roy L. Wachter

## ORION
### Floyd Root

Orion pushed ahead with his head leaning against the sharp wind and heavy falling snowflakes. The heavy hooded jacket prevented him from seeing little but the whitened ground immediately beneath his gaze. He was amazed by the contrast as an occasionally large drop of red blood marked his trail. He was not the first to be named for his place of birth. *Let's see, there's Tex, Cheyenne, Austin, oh yes, and Indiana Jones. Only he was named for a state. Or was it a University?*

He worried he would lose consciousness. *What will happen to all those people? How many will die if I am unable to arrive in time? The short cut. There has to be a short cut. I'm sure there is. But what? If I could only remember. I've got to remember the short cut. I can't quit. I can't black out again. I just can't.*

His quest had been simple enough. Until that car had pulled up. He was glad to see it slowing down. He needed a ride to get there in time. Back door opened. Man jumped out. Hit him with something, he didn't' see what it was. All he knew was, when he came to, there was a pool of blood on the snow. Searching his pockets, he found his wallet was gone. A sharp pain pounded his head. It was all he could do to remember what he was supposed to do. Had something to do with getting to Orion. An explosion of some kind. *What's that all about?* He wondered. *How can I prevent an explosion if I can't remember what it's all about? If I could only remember the shortcut, maybe that would help.*

He continued his struggle against the heavy snow fall. *What if I pass out again? What if I die? Does that mean they will all die also? I have to keep going, no matter what. I have to remember the shortcut.* It was then he bumped into a steel post, a highway sign steel post. Pain seared his head and his temples throbbed. He could feel the increase in the flow of blood from his head. His knees buckled and that was the last he remembered, at least until he came to again. He had no idea how long he had been unconscious. He could feel the pain with each pulse of his heart and his hair was wet with blood. Strangely, he felt peaceful laying there, looking up into the night sky with the moonlight shining off the heavy flakes of snow. The thought crossed his mind, *how large is the sky? Does anybody really have any idea how large the sky is? No one truly has any idea how large it is. Scientists that think they're so smart, they have no idea.* There were two steel posts holding a sign. He studied it from upside down before realizing that it proclaimed Orion, Population 1500. He smiled. *I've made it! Now to stop the explosion. I've got to remember. How can I stop anything if I can't remember? What am I supposed to do now?*

Absently mindedly, he raised his right hand, as moved by some spirit power, and allowed his arm to lie against his chest. His bare hands felt surprisingly warm. His hand lay softly on an object that was hung by a leather throng around his neck. His fingers searched out its shape, caressing it gently. *The short cut! Of course. It seemed to be coming back to him. Touch one hand to one of the steel posts supporting the Orion sign. Press the button.*

There was still much he did not understand, but that much he knew, the shortcut. He closed his eyes and prayed. *Let me be in time. All those people, they don't deserve to die like that.* He pushed the button.

Immediately, Orion disappeared into a vapor and a blue light sped into outer space, faster than the speed of light. A million times faster than the speed of light. The shortcut had worked. That night when the town was asleep, a wisp of a light flickered in the night sky. If someone had been getting a midnight drink of water, and had with sleepy eyes noticed the flicker of light, they might have thought it was nothing more than a firefly. As if there would be a firefly in the middle of a winter night. The next morning the town would awaken and no one would have any awareness that the Orion Constellation had vaporized, taking trillions of people with it.

## GHOSTS OF HOME
### Wini Fagan Frances

Twenty years can seem like an eternity. Things change. People change. And life happens. I made mistakes that cannot be undone. I needed to go back to the only home I remembered, my childhood home on the outskirts of Orion, to make things right and ask for forgiveness. Forgiveness from my parents and from the community.

On my journey back home, I focused on pleasant memories. I came up with an acrostic to help me remember. O-R-I-O-N. What would be a good O word? I settled on ORIGINAL. Unique. One-of-a-kind. That was the Orion that I knew. The town with one main paved road, a church, a school, a general store, a feed mill, a filling station, and a funeral parlor. Not too different from other small rural towns of that era. But it was its people who were original. Granny Mae waving at me every day on my way to and from school. Wilber chewing on a toothpick and sweeping the front porch of the general store. Pee Wee pumping gas and changing tires. Old maid Miss O'Rourke famous for her pinches. Pastor Henry singing off-key at the top of his voice. Walter whistling hymns while weighing the grain, and Doc who dispensed herbal remedies and ran the funeral parlor. There were others, but the most vivid positive memories are of these special people.

I thought of several different R words…risky, rowdy, ruckus, revenge, rebellion. But they described me back then, not the town. RELIGIOUS fit the town folks best. They never missed a church meeting. As many attended mid-week Bible study as did Sunday morning. Their faith in the Lord Jesus amazed me. Thinking back on their personal testimonies of how the Lord demanded their attention and how their lives changed, I wanted to believe this possibility existed for me, too. I needed faith like Granny Mae's. I remember her telling me about the struggles she faced as a young widow raising four youngsters. About her relying on the good Lord to provide the necessary food to feed her family when the cupboards were bare. Whenever I had a question, she quoted a scripture to answer it. The townspeople practiced their religion by helping those in need, reprimanding those who needed it, and loving everyone. I needed to repent and change my ways. I craved their love now. Iconic, the first word I contemplated for the letter I didn't exactly fit. Illustrious fell into the same category. I finally settled on IMPORTANT. Orion was important to me. My mom use to tell me to remember my roots, my foundation. This place helped mold me into who I am today. Reminiscing, I see how each person had an impact on my life. The folks were independent and strong, like the tree whose roots grow deep, yet bends in the storms and doesn't break. Their individuality and quirks endeared them to me. Pee Wee always shared his suckers every time Dad stopped by the station. I twisted my finger in the heavy string handle as I sucked on the purple grape ones, my favorite flavor. Then I chewed on the string to get the last bit off. I associated Wilbur with organization and cleanliness. The general store sparkled. Items were stacked precisely, each in its special spot. I remember him telling me, "Cleanliness is next to Godliness, though you can't find that verse in the Scriptures."

What would I choose for my next O word? I felt like an outcast and outsider. But that wasn't the fault of Orion. It was just my perception of things at the time. I couldn't choose opportunity, because most of the youth moved away after graduation, though some commuted to the city to work. The inhabitants of Orion were OBLIGING. Courteous, helpful, ready to serve…these all describe the businesses and people of Orion. One noticed random acts of kindness around town. The youth group mowed and raked Miss O'Rourke's yard after she fell and broke her arm. A mystery person shoveled the snow from the church sidewalk. I remember Mom taking a pot of delicious homemade chicken noodle soup and setting it on the porch by the door to Pee Wee's house so he'd see it when he walked up the road from work. She knew he couldn't afford to shut down his station when he was sick.

Now for my N word. In its natural setting of rolling hills and giant oak trees, neat and nice portray the Orion I recalled. But I opted for the word NURTURING. Doc meticulously showed and explained to us the differences in the herbs and their healing qualities. Big loving Henry, with his bear hugs for us kids, made me think of everyone's favorite grandpa. Miss O'Rourke corrected our improper grammar and stressed speaking properly. She told us we wouldn't stay in Orion forever and needed to talk like we had some upbringing, that we weren't hicks from the sticks or hillbillies. And if we didn't correct our speech when told to, she'd pinch a bit of skin and twist it. We soon learned to speak properly. Walter taught me how to whistle and let me play among the bags of feed and grain. He even helped me build forts with them. But I had to immediately report any broken bags so he could save the feed before it all spilled out.

I sang old Sunday school choruses as I drove the last fifteen miles. My palms began sweating and I used my shirt tail to wipe the steering wheel. My stomach churned. What would I find? Would my old mentors still be alive? I pulled over just before the top of the hill leading into town and said a short prayer, the first one in a long time. Then I put the car in gear, topped the hill, and gasped. I slowed to a crawl as I scanned both sides of the road. Rusted gas pumps stood as guards in front of Pee Wee's deserted station. Glass from broken windows littered the yard around the funeral parlor. An uprooted tree blocked the loading area at the feed mill. Dirt, leaves and limbs covered the front porch of the general store. Broken swings and a rusted dented slide marked the school yard. Tears streamed down my face as I stopped my car. I could barely make out Granny Mae's house and the old church in the distance.

Stumbling from my car, I continued on foot. The buckled and broken pavement made walking difficult. I tripped on a broken porch railing hiding in the tall grass and overgrowth as I stepped on Granny Mae's porch. Could I make it safely to her old rocker in the corner? Would the boards hold me? I noticed a broken rocker on the chair as I eased myself onto the damaged cane seat. What happened to the town? Why did everyone leave? There was damage, but not the kind associated with a tornado. This looked like neglect and disrepair. Memories overwhelmed me. I could almost feel Granny's arms hugging me, and whispering that everything would be okay. Nothing, no sin I'd ever committed, was too big for Jesus. He would carry my burdens if I'd only let HIM.

I felt the Holy Spirit working in my heart. The hard shell I'd built around it began to crack. Through my tears, I focused on the old clapboard church. Today the weathered boards appeared to be a dull gray, not the crisp white of my childhood. I noticed the church door stood ajar. I felt drawn to the old church. Hesitantly, I worked my way across the uneven street. The rusted hinges groaned as I pushed on the door and peeked inside. As my eyes adjusted to the dim interior, I noticed dust mites dancing in the beam of sunlight shining on the hand-carved wooden cross behind the pulpit and footprints in the dust. As I approached the cross, I remembered a memory verse I'd learned in Bible School. I pictured Pastor Henry quoting Matthew 11:28-30 with outstretched arms and looking directly at me. "Come to Me, all you who labor and are heavy laden, and I will give you rest. Take my yoke upon you and learn from Me, for I am gentle and lowly in heart, and you will find rest for your souls. For My yoke is easy and My burden is light."

With tears streaming down my face, I fell to my knees at the foot of that old rugged cross and sobbed. "Father, forgive me for turning my back on you, for even denying you when I thought it would better my chances for employment in the entertainment world. I didn't think you cared when others took advantage of my trust and inexperience. I knew you hated me when I ended up homeless and lived on the streets. I'm sorry Jesus. You didn't leave me. I left you. I realize now you were always there, leading, nudging, and guiding my footsteps back to you. If there is any way, Lord, let me find my parents and people of Orion who played such an important part in my early years. If not, I know you are my strength and shield and will never forsake me. I know you blessed me with my great voice and singing ability, Lord. From now on, I will use it to glorify you. In Jesus name, I pray. Amen."

God's grace. I felt it once again as I repented and gave my life back to Jesus. I felt free of my burden of sin and broke out in song. I faced the cross with outstretched arms and sang, "Amazing grace, how sweet the sound, that saved a wretch like me. I once was lost, but now am found. Was blind, but now I..." A board creaked, and I heard beautiful harmony joining in as I sang "see."

I twirled around and stared into the expressive, compassionate brown eyes of Granny's oldest grandson, Peter. I threw my arms around him, stood on tiptoe, kissed his cheek, and buried my head in his chest. "Rachel! Is it really you? I'd know your voice anywhere." Happy tears trickled down my cheeks as I nodded. "You know, Granny never quit praying for you. And neither did I." His arms tightened around me as I heard him whisper, "Thank you, God, for bringing her home safe."

When I finally gained control of myself, I asked him about the town and the people. What had happened? We sat on the front pew holding hands as he told me about the coal mine closing. This had a ripple effect. Because there was no more money in the community, the businesses closed. Property values plummeted. The folks exited to the nearby city with all its amenities. "Because the town was deserted, the land was cheap. I purchased the whole town, all the buildings and all twenty acres, for $60,000. I have just started cleaning the place up. Come see my first project."

Peter led me behind the church. No weeds grew in the cemetery. He had mowed and trimmed around each headstone. It seemed strange to me that the cemetery was the only place that showed any sign of life and renewal. I looked at him and smiled. That was the Peter I remembered…caring, respectful, and grounded in faith and family.

"Have you seen your parents, yet?" As I shook my head no, he continued. "That was a crazy question, wasn't it? I understand you've had no contact with them for twenty years. You wouldn't know where they live now. Come. Let me take you to your parents. And tomorrow we'll go visit Granny Mae in the nursing home. She leads a Bible study group at 10:00.

As we headed toward Peter's pickup hand in hand, I thought of many more questions that needed answered, but they could wait awhile longer. Right now, I was going home.

Made in the USA
Middletown, DE
23 September 2015